CHEATER, CHEATER, PUMPKIN EATER

CHEATER, CHEATER, PUMPKIN EATER

AUSTIN MOON

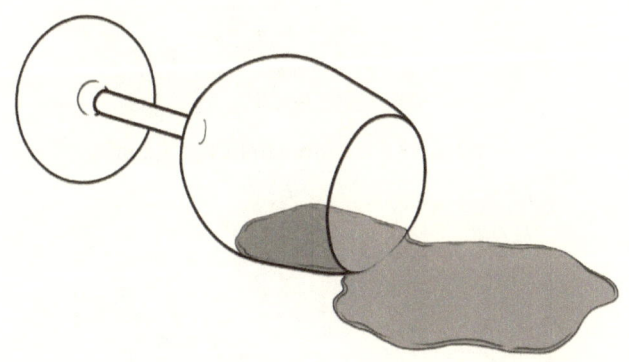

Cheater, Cheater, Pumpkin Eater. Copyright © 2025 by Austin Moon.

Triomphe Press 2025

Cover illustration and design by Austin Moon

ISBN 978-1-958123-16-4

First Edition: June 2025

Printed in the United States of America

10 9 8 7 6 5 4 3 2

Grammy, thanks for being one of my biggest supporters

PROLOGUE

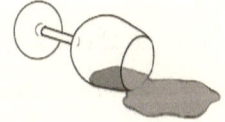

As Robert got out of the car his phone began to ring. He braced for impact, worried it might be his wife, but the caller ID showed it was Kobayashi's—his favorite sushi place in East Hollywood.

Robert grinned. "Why are you calling me? I just left the theater, baby. You can't stand to be away from me for more than ten minutes?" He said it as if he was annoyed, however he secretly enjoyed the constant attention, the admiration.

The caller said something in return that made Robert chuckle. "I know, I know. That is what I said, didn't I? Well, don't worry, baby. Everything is going exactly how we planned it. She doesn't suspect a thing." He shook his head and leaned against the side of the BMW sitting in the driveway. "No, no, I know. A couple more weeks. Then it will all be over. I promise." He smiled.

The sound of the front door opening made him instantly school his features. "Gotta go." He hung up the phone and shoved it deep in his pocket.

Caroline leaned out the doorway and caught his gaze. "Why are you standing around outside? It's cold."

He plastered on a grin. "I like the cold, Caroline. Because then, when you get inside, you can appreciate how warm it is."

She looked at him as if it was the strangest thing she'd ever heard him say and shook her head slightly. "Okay, Robert. Just don't catch the flu. I can't afford to get sick right now. Our newest campaign is going to be our biggest rollout to date, and I have to fly to New York this week."

He smiled even wider. "Don't worry, Caroline. I won't get you sick. *Promise.*"

ONE

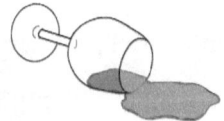

When I entered the office Dean and Lexi were sword fighting. Dean was using a broom handle, and Lexi—who had a much bigger advantage since she'd actually *taken* fencing lessons—was using a long stick my black labradoodle, Captain, had brought back from his walk that morning.

Lexi attacked, and Dean parried—stepping one foot back and getting it inadvertently stuck in the waste bin.

"What the hell is going on?" I put my hands on my hips for maximum emphasis.

Lexi grinned, victorious, while Dean cringed like a kid who'd been caught stealing candy. "Nothing," he said. "It's not what it looks like."

Lexi poked Dean in the chest with her *sword*, securing her a point. "It's *exactly* what it looks like, actually."

Dean shrugged. "Well, yes, technically. But if you want to look at it from a different perspective..."

I waited for him to finish his sentence and realized he had nothing. I pointed at Lexi. "*You* are supposed to be studying for your finals. And *you*," I pointed at Dean, "are supposed to be finding us a case. We haven't had anything good in the last two weeks. One lost dog and an old lady afraid someone is peeping into her windows is *not* going to pay the bills."

I sighed. Our success in returning an Egyptian antiquity for Dean's fake uncle—*long story*—and solving two murders committed by a mob boss's power-hungry daughter was supposed to bring us new, rich clients. It hadn't helped at all.

I'd let the lead police detective on the case, Detective Warner, get all the credit to keep Dean out of the hot seat when I'd discovered he had a criminal past that painted a target on his back. However, we could have used that good press. All we'd gotten was a brief mention in some online article. Hardly anything to write home about. Now the agency was stuck in the same rut as before. Only, two weeks ago I hadn't been paying Dean as my new assistant investigator. He'd been the one paying *me*.

I was so desperate for cash I was even toying with the idea of asking my parents for money. Which was my absolute worst nightmare. Having my parents, who already thought my being a private detective was the stupidest decision I'd ever made, potentially turning me down? I'd rather beg on the streets than live through that humiliation. I needed a case to work and I needed it now.

Dean smiled, pulling his foot out of the waste bin and brushing his dark locks back up into their neat styling. "Ah, but there's where you're wrong, detective." He waggled his stick-sword in my direction.

I narrowed my eyes. "Wrong *how* exactly?" As far as I was aware, we were dead in the water client-wise.

He straightened up his suit jacket. Today it was gray with pink pinstripes. "I got us a client." He cocked his head to the side and shrugged. "Well, a potential client."

Lexi scoffed and said, "*Potential client,*" before sitting down in her usual seat behind the front desk. She pushed her long dark hair over her shoulder and waited for him to continue.

I crossed my arms and walked over to him. "You did?"

He laughed through his nose. "Don't sound so surprised."

"But I am." I smiled and raised an eyebrow. "Who's the client?"

Dean practiced his fencing lunges with his stick, his gaze locked onto the sofa he was currently murdering. "An old friend of mine I met at the club a few years ago. I play golf with her and her husband every so often. Caroline Foil."

"I see. So they're marks of yours?"

Dean abandoned his fencing and placed his hand on his chest in faux outrage, looking me dead in the eye. "Of course not. Can't I just play golf with a rich, older couple without scrutiny?"

"*No,*" I deadpanned, reaching for his stick-sword and putting it to the side before he hurt himself.

He rolled his eyes. "Fine, I *may* have been courting them a little bit for a deal I was working on, but I never acted on it. I do have my standards, you know? I only go after the smarmy, selfish type. And Caroline may be old money, but she's really kind. And she uses her wealth wisely."

"What does she do?" I'd never heard of her.

He gestured with his hand, looking away. "She runs a major fashion magazine—Runway magazine."

I narrowed my eyes. "That's using her money *wisely*?"

He tutted his tongue. "She's on the board of *three* massive humanitarian charities, Noah. A large chunk of her money goes towards doing good and making change."

"How'd she make all that money?" I asked.

He shrugged. "*Hmm,* I think her grandparents made most of it during the war, planes or something."

I sighed. "*Okay,* so she's not an *evil* millionaire, then. What does she want to hire us for?"

He shook his head. "She didn't say over the phone. We're meeting her for lunch at the club to discuss the case."

Lexi piped up, "Do you think she's serious about it? Because looking at the books, we can't go on much longer without some new clients. Rent is due."

Thanks Lexi, ever the optimist.

Dean grinned. "Caroline is always serious. She wouldn't ask us to meet her if she didn't need the help."

"Okay, when and where?" I asked, pulling around the front desk to check our paper calendar—not that there was anything we needed to schedule *around*.

Dean tapped his finger on the desk. "Today, an hour from now."

I scoffed. "You couldn't have given me some time to prepare?"

He shrugged. "Rich people have tight schedules and even stricter expectations. It was either now or never."

"Fine." I let out a deep sigh, resigned.

"You'll need a suit," Lexi added, looking me up and down. I was wearing my usual outfit of dark khakis and a matching t-shirt. I'd ditched my go-to leather jacket as the Los Angeles spring weather grew hotter and hotter.

"Oh, right." I visualized my bedroom closet that was one floor above the office. "I think my only suit was shredded from the last time we went to the golf club."

Dean frowned. "You mean when my Speedster met her untimely end?"

During our last case the killer had tried to blow up Dean's car with us inside. We narrowly escaped becoming barbecue. The car, not so much. "That too," I said.

Dean patted my shoulder. "That's okay, you can borrow one of mine."

Lexi laughed.

"*What?*" I glared at her.

She shook her head and covered her smile with her hand. "No offense, Uncle Noah, but I don't think you're Dean's size."

I pulled my shoulders back and straightened my spine. "What do you mean?" I looked between myself and Dean. "We're close enough."

Dean grinned and then winked at Lexi. "Don't worry, I have a couple *looser* suit jackets from when Fern and I lived in Italy for a summer. It's all about loose over there."

I was still getting used to the fact that Dean's closest friend and roommate, Felicity, was actually named Fern. Another thing on the long list that they'd lied to me about.

I lowered my brows and pressed my lips together into a thin line. "Let's stop having this conversation before I fire both of you."

They laughed together at my expense as I walked across the office to the front door. I looked back. "Coming?"

What Dean picked out for me was *not* what I would have called *loose*. It was uncomfortably tight in the shoulders and armpits, and every time I buttoned the waist it popped open again.

Dean looked me up and down as we walked toward the clubhouse from the parking lot—we'd skipped valet today. "You look fine."

I frowned. "What a great adjective, thanks."

He jogged to catch up to me and patted my stomach. "Just suck it in for a few minutes and then when we sit you can unbutton it again."

I scoffed. "It's not my fault you have a freakish shoulder-to-waist ratio. Not everyone can look like a cover model. My stomach is just fine the way it is, un-sucked."

He grinned, revealing white teeth, clearly amused at my outburst. "I can see I've hit a nerve. Ignore me."

"*Gladly.*"

I brushed my buzzed hair with my hand to try and tame it, though what was the point? It only looked one way.

We entered the lobby and I followed Dean across the plush gold carpet to the club's restaurant. The large wall of windows that overlooked the golf course lit up the room with afternoon sunlight. Dean whispered something to the host behind the host stand, and we were ushered across the space to a table in the back. I couldn't help but notice that the room was fairly empty, so the choice to seat us in the darkest corner was deliberate.

A woman in her fifties with a sharp, platinum blonde bob was already sitting down at the table, a glass of glistening ice water in front of her.

Dean grinned. "Caroline, nice to see you."

She rose from her seat and kissed his cheek. "Dean, it's been forever."

"It has, too long. Caroline, this is the detective I was telling you about, Noah Sun."

She smiled at me. "Nice to meet you, Mr. Sun." She gestured to the empty seats. "Please, gentlemen, sit down."

We sat across from her at the round table. A waitress materialized and filled our water glasses and handed us thin, glossy menus.

Now that we were situated and the niceties were out of the way, Caroline had a strained expression on her face, her lips pinched and her brows drawn. "Thank you for meeting me here at the club."

Dean grinned genially. "Of course."

Caroline waved her hand through the air. "Normally I would have invited you to join me at my office. I just can't guarantee it would be completely private. I love my employees, however they have sharp ears and even sharper tongues." She lowered her voice to a whisper. "At least here at the club I can ensure they'll be discreet with a little extra cash."

Rich people.

I leaned in. "Are you worried about your employees? Is that why you want to hire us?" I asked.

She shook her head. "No, not at all. This is a completely personal matter." She turned to Dean. "I think Robert is cheating on me."

If Dean had been the type to gasp, right then would have been the time to do it. His eyes widened a fraction, instead.

Dean reached out his hand across the intimate white-clothed table. "I'm sorry, Caroline."

"What makes you suspect he's having an affair?" I asked, all business. I was used to having this exact conversation, and it usually went one of two ways. It was either painfully obvious that their partner was cheating and they simply needed documented proof for their lawyer, *or* the client in question had a million small pieces of *evidence* that weren't really evidence of anything at all. On the surface, Caroline didn't strike me as the type to be paranoid that her husband was cheating, though.

I pulled out my notebook from my inner jacket pocket and had my pen poised to write.

Caroline sighed and hung her head. "He's been lying to me about where he is. He keeps telling me that he's working late at the theater, but every time I try and call him his phone is conveniently off and nobody at the theater can locate him. Not to mention the money."

"The money?" I asked.

She nodded, clasping her hands across the table. "Every time I check our bank statements there's all these odd charges. I almost called the bank to have them cancel Robert's card, thinking it must have been stolen, when there were charges for restaurants and shops in Orange County. Robert told me that he'd needed to go there unexpectedly for business." She shook her head. "There's no reason anything at the theater would cause him to buy gifts at a women's boutique in Newport Beach. They're such stupid lies."

I agreed that the lies were stupid, unfortunately I'd seen worse in other cases. Cheaters weren't particularly bright. "Okay, and what would you like us to do?" I asked.

She grew serious, pressing her lips together and narrowing her eyes. She leaned forward. "I want you to catch the bastard. I need photographic proof. I worked too hard to have my whole empire put under legal scrutiny when I file for divorce. Robert is selfish, I know him. If I confront him now he'll drag me to court and try to take more than his fair share. I was stupid and young when I married him. I should have had a prenup written like my mother had always wanted. I was too spiteful back then."

She gestured toward Dean. "You'll remember that I loaned Robert his start-up capital to buy the theater. I supported him through that crucial first year where he actually *lost* money."

"Do you know who the other woman is?" Dean asked quietly, though there was no one around to listen in. The bartender was minding his own business across the room from us—wiping down glasses—and our waitress was nowhere to be seen.

She nodded. "Camila Martinez. At least I *suspect* that's who it is. She's in Robert's newest play, the one about the suffragettes. She's the lead, very pretty."

"Is there anything in particular that makes you believe it's her?" I asked. That was a pretty big guess.

She gave me a hardened stare. "There's been rumors going around the theater. And I know my husband, Mr. Sun. I know what he likes. She's a petite brunette with certain...assets."

I couldn't help but notice the woman she was describing sounded like the total opposite of Caroline who was tall, lithe, and blonde.

"Okay, that's a good starting point," Dean said.

She looked down at her lap and pulled a folded up piece of paper from her purse. "He's going to be in Newport again this weekend and I know he'll be with her. I have his hotel details written down here. You have my permission to do whatever you need to do. And I'll pay your full rate. Extra if you can get both their faces clearly in the shot. I want to prove beyond a doubt that I'm right." She slid the paper across the table to us.

I cleared my throat. "I always have to ask—are you sure you want to do this? Yes, you have your theories now, but once we find proof, there's no going back from that."

Caroline looked me straight in the eye. "I'm sure."

"Okay." I nodded. "Then we'll get started on this immediately. I'll have my assistant send you an invoice for the deposit. How would you like us to send that?"

"Don't send it to the office," she said sternly. "I don't want anyone knowing about this. Total privacy."

"Don't worry, Ms. Foil. We're very discreet at The Golden Sun Detective Agency ."

Dean smiled and grabbed Caroline's hand across the table. "We'll do anything we can to help."

She shook her head, her eyes going glassy, but no tears were allowed to fall. "It happens, right? Every day."

Dean nodded. "That doesn't make it any easier."

She let out a long held breath and looked down at the table. "I need to get back to the office. I've already instructed the club staff to charge this meal to my account, so please stay and have lunch. I'll wire you the deposit as soon as I get your email." She rose from her seat and grabbed her purse from the back of the chair.

"Thank you, Ms. Foil," I added.

She nodded, not really looking at either of us. "Turns out twenty years of marriage isn't good for much anymore. I swear if Robert didn't need my money for that damn theater of his he'd have gotten rid of me a long time ago."

Neither of us knew what to say to that, so it hung in the silence until Caroline turned to leave. "Have a nice lunch, boys. When you have something worth showing me, come by the house. Dean knows the place."

"Will do." Dean smiled and waved as she walked away, not looking back again.

"Dang," I said after she left. "Cheating cases are always intense, but this one feels *particularly* charged."

Dean shook his head. "It was always hard to get a good read on their relationship. The two of them kept their personal life so private I guess I never really saw the cracks. Even so, it doesn't exactly surprise me. I never understood what Caroline and Robert had in common. Robert is...an odd guy. I don't know."

"*Hmm.*" My phone buzzed and I checked it to find that I had a text from my mother asking me if I had time this week to come by the house. What she really wanted was to berate me about my career choices and money problems, as usual. No thanks. I deleted the message. She could wait until we finished this job.

I took a sip of my water and noticed Dean slip something into his jacket pocket. "What did you just take?" I furrowed my brow. "Did you just steal some silverware?"

He scoffed and narrowed his eyes. "Are you serious, Noah?"

"I'm just asking, I know you like to take things that aren't yours," I said. "I thought we had an agreement? No more conning or stealing and in exchange you get to work for me, earn some honest income."

He pulled his hand out from his pocket and placed the item on the table. "I was grabbing a complimentary breath mint, not The Hope Diamond. Can you chill, please?"

I stared at the plastic wrapped mint and squirmed, my neck flushing with heat. I realized how stupid the accusation was. "I'm...sorry, Dean. I guess I'm feeling a little on edge today." I sighed. "We've had virtually no clients for the past two weeks and now this case comes along, and it should be easy-peasy—I've worked a million of these cheating scandals, only this one feels different." Not to mention my parents always breathing down my neck, reminding me what a disappointment I was.

His face relaxed, and he squeezed my shoulder. "It'll be fine. Caroline is just going through a hard time. I'm sure once we get to Newport you'll be all work and no play like usual."

I frowned. "*I play.*"

He raised a brow. "When do you play? Because for the past three weeks that I've known you, you haven't done anything I would call *fun.*"

I laughed through my nose. "Maybe we just have different definitions of the word."

He rolled his eyes and took a sip of his water. "That's why you need me, Noah. You need to broaden your horizons, get a new perspective. Live a little."

I rolled my too-tight shoulders, the borrowed suit suddenly feeling *extra* snug around my frame. "I don't *need* you." Just because Dean was working with me now didn't mean that I *needed* him.

"Fine, but I'm nice to have around," he argued.

I shrugged. "Debatable."

"Oh my God, are you incapable of giving me any sort of compliment?" Dean said it lightheartedly, but I could tell I'd genuinely offended him.

I pinched my brows together. "Sorry, I didn't mean it like that. I just meant, you're still new, is all. You're not a detective yet."

He beamed. "*Yet* being the operative word in that sentence."

I let out a breath and laughed.

"Now, can we have a nice lunch before getting back to the grind, *Mr. Grumps*?" he asked, unfolding his cloth napkin and dropping it in his lap.

I nodded and picked up the forgotten menu from the table. "Yes, Dean. Let's have lunch."

He waved his hand through the air. "After all, you can't catch cheating husbands on an empty stomach."

I chuckled. "No, no you can't."

TWO

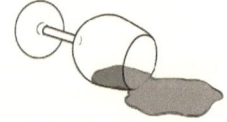

"I'm bored," Dean said before pouting in a way that I imagined a small child would.

I sighed and leaned back against the Jeep's headrest. The Vanguard Hotel in Newport was busy with weekend guests, so nobody bothered us across the street. "Hi Bored, I'm Noah. How's it going?"

His lips twitched. "Did you just make a joke?"

I narrowed my eyes and crossed my arms. "What do you mean? I make jokes all the time."

Dean shook his head and laughed. "Right, okay."

"I'm *very* funny." I didn't know why I felt the need to defend myself, and yet I kept going.

"Sure."

I sighed. "You are so annoying sometimes. Can't we just sit in silence like normal private investigators during a stakeout?"

He laughed. "How do you know they're all silent? How many other private investigators do you even know? Is there a club you can join?"

I shrugged, my eyes skating over the dark hotel room window. "A few." It was true, I had a small network of other investigators I could call on if things got really dicey. However, I usually found a way to handle things on my own.

Dean hummed. "Have you ever thought about the idea that maybe actually *you're* the weirdo?"

I narrowed my eyes. "No, thank you for that helpful insight. I see the situation in a whole new light."

He grinned. "Really?"

"No, of course not. Now, pay attention."

He sighed. "I *am* paying attention. I see the same empty hotel room that you see, Noah. At what point do we do something here?"

I glanced over at him. "Like what exactly?"

He gestured toward the building. "Like *wait inside*, for instance."

I shook my head. "Bad idea. Just because a subject doesn't know who you are, doesn't mean that you want them to see you. That's last resort. Especially in this type of case."

He shook his head. "What type of case?"

I waved my hand. "You know, cheating. That's why we're all the way in Newport. People who have affairs want to be out in the open. If they feel like they're being watched they clam up. We want to lull them into a false sense of security."

Dean blew out a slow breath. "Well the only person you're currently lulling, is me...to sleep."

I glared at him. "This is the job, Dean. You can leave at any time if you don't want to be here."

He huffed out a breath and slid down in his seat. "All right, all right, I'm watching." He crossed his arms and continued staring at the dark hotel window.

He was right about one thing: our subjects were late. Whatever information Caroline had obtained from Robert hadn't come to fruition as of yet. They *were* staying at the hotel that night, that much was certain. It was easy to talk the front desk clerk into confirming they'd checked in earlier that day. As easy as twenty dollars slipped across the desk. It was also simple enough to tip a housekeeper into opening the curtains in their room.

Now it was the boring task of waiting for the couple to return and get to business. If they decided to close the curtains again we'd have to switch to plan B, which would take much longer and be much more annoying: follow them. That would make Dean happy. Which would make me *unhappy*.

I checked my watch—ten o'clock. It was still early for the weekend crowd, but Robert's reservation at the restaurant down the street had been for four hours ago.

The loud thrum of a European sports car made me look up. The neon blue model pulled under the covered valet drop-off in front of the entrance to the hotel. A man in his fifties with salt and pepper hair slipped out and pulled the passenger side door open for a woman with long dark waves wearing a fiery red dress.

"Dean." I nudged his shoulder.

"What?" he asked in a bored monotone.

"That's them."

He jerked his head up to look at the couple next to the car. "What? Why the hell is he showing up in a Maserati? I thought you said cheaters were only comfortable when they weren't being watched? That car draws so much attention to them."

"I did say that. This is a bit strange, but people are sometimes unpredictable. Get the camera ready, we're about to get our money shot."

Dean lifted the camera from his lap and turned it on, messing with the heavy zoom lens. "What if we don't get any pictures? Has that ever happened to you before?"

I turned to him and smirked. "Never." Dean rolled his eyes. "But if it *does* happen, we can always try again. That's all a part of the job."

The couple stood outside the front entrance for a few minutes, Robert's hand on the small of Camilla's back.

"God, this is so weird." Dean sneered at them, his eyes narrowed. "I thought he loved Caroline, in his own way at least."

I shrugged. "Maybe he still does. Love is complicated."

He scoffed. "Not *that* complicated. You don't just abandon a partner at the first sign of trouble, and with your *employee* of all people. What a gross dynamic." He seemed to rethink his words as he turned to look at my face. I'd kissed him when Dean was just a client, and now he was *my* employee. "I must sound like a broken record, cheating is bad, *blah, blah, blah.*"

I smiled. "I didn't say cheating wasn't bad, I just said that relationships are complicated and they often have many twists and turns that you don't expect. You can never really know someone completely. Getting into a relationship is a gamble. Sometimes it doesn't work out and you get hurt."

I wondered if *I* sounded like a broken record now. Dean hadn't known me when I was engaged to my ex, Malcolm. He only knew the Noah that had come after.

"*Huh*, I suppose you're right." Dean pointed across the car, through the window. "They're going inside."

I grabbed his arm and pulled it down. "What did I tell you about pointing?"

He cringed. "That it's rude?"

"Ninety percent of surveillance is not drawing attention to yourself," I reminded him.

"But at least I'm good at the other ten percent?" Dean offered with a smirk.

"Just stay ready. They could make it up there any second." We trained our eyes to the window on the second floor. The angle was odd, but with the hotel sitting on a hill we could still see inside fairly well. These photographs weren't going to win any awards for artistic composition, but they'd get the job done.

We waited for a few minutes in silence.

"There." The light turned on in the room. The blinds weren't fully open—that would have been too obvious—they were only half-drawn. Robert walked in front of the glass, his frame shadowed by the lights.

"How long does it usually—" The question died on Dean's lips as Robert pulled off his shirt. "*Oh.*"

"Yeah, not long." The scene was picture perfect, the couple silhouetted against the window. "Pictures!" I bumped Dean's shoulder, and he sprung into action, lifting the camera to his line of sight. The shutter clicked as picture after picture was captured.

"Is this damning enough?" Dean asked, pulling the camera down to look at the screen.

"Yeah, I'd say so." I checked the preview image. "We don't need to stick around for the show. Two people shirtless in each other's arms, what else could they possibly be doing? Running lines?"

Being in the same quiet car with Dean again, watching the couple go at it, made my neck flush. It reminded me of when *we'd* kissed in this same car not two weeks ago. That had been a mistake. Like I'd told Dean before—he was my employee now. And even if that wasn't the case, I didn't mix business with my personal life. I'd tried that already with Malcolm, and I couldn't go down that road again. It had led to a very messy, painful end.

As if on cue, a hand reached out and pulled the curtains closed. It didn't matter. We'd gotten what we'd come for.

"Is that it?" Dean asked, looking through the images on the camera screen.

I shrugged. "Yeah, generally. We give the photos to Caroline and then we move on to the next case."

"That was surprisingly easy," Dean said with a satisfied smile.

I laughed through my nose. "I told you. When people feel like they're not being watched they get cocky. Robert was the one who made it so easy. He was totally brazen—the car, the restaurant, the hotel."

"*Hmm.*" Dean nodded. "Poor Caroline, though."

I started the Jeep and clicked on my seatbelt. "Poor Caroline indeed."

THREE

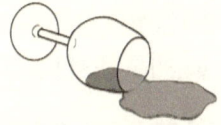

Early the next morning, I stood outside Dean's apartment door. The real one on the east side of LA, not the downtown luxury suite that he'd claimed to live in weeks before I knew who he truly was. My jacket pocket was weighed down, and my heart was hammering in my chest. I wiped off my sweaty palms and knocked on the door.

Fern answered a few seconds later. She looked like she was ready for a tropical resort wearing a flowy chiffon lounge set and sunglasses. "Oh, Noah, nice to see you again. Dean told me all about your trip last night."

I smiled and walked inside. "He did, did he?"

She gestured with a manicured hand. "Honestly, even if it is a large pay cut, I think Dean is really enjoying this new career path he's chosen."

I furrowed my brow. "As opposed to your previous career path of lying and stealing?"

She waved away the criticism. "All in the past, darling." She turned to call over her shoulder. "Dean, your detective is here."

I wasn't *his* detective, but I didn't say that.

Dean sauntered into the room wearing a blue suit fit for spring, paired with a mustard yellow tie. "Do you think this is appropriate for giving bad news?" he asked, his brows knit with worry. "Or is it *good* news, technically?"

I shrugged. "It's news, whether she likes it or not. You look...nice."

He beamed, showing off his Crest smile. "Thanks, detective." Dean kissed Fern on the cheek. "I'll be back for dinner, hopefully. Don't wait up for me, darling."

She laughed. "I never do."

I followed Dean out the door and down the hall. "So, Fern looks to be doing well. What's she doing lately?" She used to be a con man (con woman?), now she'd joined Dean in turning their lives around.

Dean laughed. "Believe it or not she's a fashion designer's muse right now."

I raised a brow. "Is that a lucrative job?"

He shrugged one shoulder. "She gets paid in clothes and free gift bags, which isn't ideal, but that's what Ebay is for. I think she's having a blast. She told me to give her two more weeks and she'd be running the fashion house herself."

"I don't doubt that." Fern was cunning and extremely capable. She was a large part of the reason their conning double act had been successful for so long.

As soon as we got to the Jeep I was reminded of the package in my chest pocket, the corner digging into my sternum. "I uh...have something for you," I said quietly, looking down at the dash.

Dean turned to me with raised brows and wide eyes. "You do?"

I held my twitchy, nervous hands down in my lap. "It's nothing important. I just thought since you're new at the agency you deserved a small welcome gift, that's all."

He beamed. "Really?"

"See, now you're building it up in your mind, but it's just a small, little thing." I shook my head. "I also just wanted to...apologize for what I said yesterday at the club. I wasn't trying to imply that I don't trust you. I know you're not some simple thief for hire. I don't know why I accused you of stealing that cutlery. It was stupid of me," I said all in a rush.

He raised an eyebrow. "Glad to know we're on the same page, detective."

We sat in silence for a few painful seconds.

He laughed. "So, are you going to give me the gift, or do I have to steal it from your jacket pocket?"

"Oh, uh." I slipped the small black box from its hiding spot and held it out. "How did you know it was there?" I asked.

One side of his mouth raised and he said, "Old habits." He took the box and rolled it in his hands slowly. "What could it be?"

I waved my hand. "Oh, just open it, Dean."

"Why?" He smirked. "I like watching you squirm."

I frowned, which made him laugh. "Okay, okay, I'm opening it." He lifted the lid off the box and pulled the tissue paper aside. In the center of the box was a ring. A simple gold band with a small red stone embedded at the top. "A ring?" His face pinched with confusion, and then morphed into joy. "Are you proposing to me, detective? "

"*Uh, er.*" I stumbled to speak. "No. *Definitely not.*"

He gave me a strange look and then glanced down at the box again. "Oh, I see now. It's not a typical ring." He picked it up and played with it for a second, discovering the mechanism that made the blade pop open. His eyes widened. "That's terrific, thanks."

I tried not to blush as he messed with the blade. "I figured as my new employee you needed something to protect yourself with when I wasn't around. It's probably not really your style, but I know how you like nice things."

He peered up, caught my eye, and smirked. "What makes you think I need protecting? I can take care of myself. I have so far."

"Well, all the same. It might come in handy."

He grinned. "Thanks, I appreciate it."

I nodded and started the car. "Anyway, let's get to it. Caroline is expecting those photos." I gestured to the folder of glossy photographs that sat on the dash.

"Right." He slipped the ring onto his pointer finger. I must have done a good enough job at guessing his size because it fit perfectly.

Good. That was done. Now on to the real work.

* * *

Caroline's house was up in the hills—of course. It sat on a ridge by itself at the top of a long drive. The place was all modern glass and white concrete. Very typical for the LA elite. I imagined she'd owned it for a while, but the house was manicured and power washed, so everything looked fresh and expensive. There was only one car in the driveway—Robert would still be in Newport this morning as far as Caroline had told us. I'd asked the staff to call me if they left early, and I hadn't received any news, so I was assuming that it was still true.

I buzzed the call box that sat in front of the black iron gate and waited for a response. Nothing. "She did say ten, didn't she?" I asked, though I was positive I'd remembered correctly.

Dean nodded. "Yeah, she's very particular about time, she wouldn't forget.

I buzzed again and still got no response.

Dean sighed. "Try 9–8-4-5-2-3."

I gave him a funny look. "And you would know this how?"

He shrugged one shoulder. "I just remembered it from the last time I was here with Caroline."

He remembered a number he saw one time maybe six months ago? I stored that information away in my brain and punched in the code. The call box beeped and the iron gate began to retract. "Well let's hope she doesn't mind that you happen to know the code to her home."

Dean waved his hand nonchalantly. "We can just say the gate was already open."

I scoffed. "What a great legal defense."

He narrowed his eyes at me as I drove up to the front of the house and parked behind Caroline's Range Rover. I grabbed the folder off the dash as we got out of the car and walked up to the large, frosted glass front door.

I rang the doorbell—it was one of those expensive types with the live camera feed you could see on your phone. And then we waited. And waited. No sound from inside, no sign someone was around.

"I mean, her car is here, so she must be home, right?" Dean asked, trying his best to look through the opaque glass of the door.

"Probably," I said, "but you know rich people. She might have a second car."

He shook his head. "She wouldn't forget our meeting, though. She's too type A for that."

I took a few steps back and surveyed the house. "So what do you want to do?"

Dean was already walking, making his way around the side of the house to the side gate. It was unlocked and cracked open.

"Are you sure you want to go snooping around?" I called out. "This could get very awkward if she just overslept or something."

Dean frowned and narrowed his eyes. "I don't know, I'm getting a bad feeling, Noah. This is out of character for Caroline."

I nodded and followed his lead. Caroline was *his* friend, not mine. We slipped past the gate and walked down the cement and glass tile walkway toward the backyard. We passed bushes of spring flowers trimmed to round button shapes and drought-tolerant desert plants like aloe and cacti surrounded by lava rock.

"Oh my God." Dean stopped in front of me, and I bumped into him. I had to grab his shoulders so I didn't fall over.

"What?" I spotted the issue immediately. Face down, floating in the olympic-sized swimming pool, was Caroline Foil.

* * *

Dean took a seat on one of the many Adirondack lounge chairs while we waited for the police to respond to my call. This wasn't his first dead body, however Caroline was his friend.

She was wearing a pale silk nightgown, and her blonde hair was in a halo around her head. Nothing else was in the pool—no phone, no wineglass, no chair.

"I don't understand," he said, his eyes trained on his hands. "What happened?"

I was bad at comforting people, so I decided to go with the facts. That always helped *me* when I needed to calm down. "Well, I see three options here."

He looked up at my face.

"One: it was an accident. Maybe she hit her head or accidentally fell in the pool and then panicked."

"Okay."

I nodded. "Option two: she did it on purpose. Even without our photos she knew her husband was cheating on her and she couldn't stomach it, so she took her own life."

Dean was already shaking his head. "She wouldn't do that."

"And finally option three: someone did this *to* her."

He bit his lip. "And which one do you think is most likely?"

"Well." I sat down next to him in the matching lounge chair. "I didn't know her like you did, but if I had to make a guess? I'd probably say it was an accident. Do you feel up to looking around inside? Before the cops get here?"

He furrowed his brow and nodded. "Yeah, let's do that."

I wrapped my arm around his shoulders as we stood up, and I led him toward the back of the house. The glass patio door was wide open. How long had she been floating in the pool? It was hard to know only by what she looked like, but from the nightgown I'd hazard a guess that it had been at least a few hours. Maybe late last night? We'd messaged her about the photos around ten thirty, so it had to have been sometime after that.

The inside of the house was just as stunning as the outside. It looked more like a model home in some architecture magazine than a real lived-in space. The whites and grays were calming, yet dull. I'd hate to drink red wine in a place like this. The anxiety it would bring.

"Look." Dean pointed toward the massive white marble island in the kitchen. Two empty bottles of white wine sat there along with an empty overturned wineglass.

"Is that a normal amount of wine for Caroline?" I asked.

Dean shrugged. "I mean, she definitely liked her daily glass of wine, but two bottles? I don't know."

The kitchen was otherwise surgically clean. Nothing amiss there.

"Do you hear that?" Dean asked, his head cocked to the side in concentration.

"What?" There was a faint chirping noise, coming from where?

Dean pointed towards the ceiling. "Upstairs."

I followed Dean up the grand staircase and down a hallway. The chirping grew louder and more obvious that it was a dog barking. We stopped in front of the door at the end of the hall. There was an animal scratching on the other side, clawing to get out. "Don't open it," I instructed.

"Why?" Dean asked.

"Because even if you know that dog, they could still bite you." I pondered the dog in the locked room. "Either Caroline put the dog up here by itself because she had company coming over, or someone else stuck the dog inside to keep it out of the way."

"Maybe she was just annoyed and wanted some time alone?" Dean added. "Or maybe she was afraid the dog was going to jump in the pool and drown since she had the back door wide open?"

"*Hmm.*" I shook my head. "I don't know, it seems like an odd thing to do when you're by yourself."

"Let's go look downstairs some more. We're running out of time."

He was right about that. I checked my watch. It had already been five minutes. The police would be here any second. Even up in the hills they were pretty fast. "Okay, let's hustle." We dashed downstairs and searched. It was easy to search a space that was so meticulously organized. Any disorder popped out immediately. "There, the coffee table," I said. On the glass coffee table was a small, white oval-shaped pill. Dumped out onto the wooden floor was the rest of the bottle. I crouched down and read the label. "Sleeping pills." The nasty, murderous kind. "Do you know if she took these regularly?"

Dean shook his head slowly. "Possibly? She did mention she had trouble sleeping once. She was stressed out from her job at the magazine."

I stood up and walked over to Dean. "I'm not gonna lie, it's looking like a strong case for option two."

Dean gaped. "Suicide? I can't imagine Caroline doing that. *Especially* over Robert. You heard her the other day at the club. She was preparing to fight. She was strong. Why would she suddenly give up?"

I crossed my arms. "Maybe it all got to be too much. Or maybe I'm reading this wrong and it *was* option one. She was drinking and she took a sleeping pill or two, and she accidentally fell into the pool. No one was here to help her, and then she drowned."

Dean pressed his lips together, his brows pinched. "I don't like any of these options."

I reached out and squeezed his shoulder. "I know. I'm sorry, Dean. Hopefully this is an open and shut case and we can move on quickly."

The sirens grew louder as the cops reached the front gate. "I better go open that for them." Dean was about to speak, but I cut him off. "I remember the code. That's going to be fun to explain to them how we got in here to find her body."

I left Dean inside and went to let the police into the driveway. I recognized two of the officers. They seemed surprised to see me. "Rough day?" an officer named Bennet asked as she entered the house.

"I'd say so." I pointed them to the backyard through the open door.

"Have you touched anything?" another officer asked.

I shook my head. "Nothing. The crime scene is clean."

He nodded. "Good."

We had to stand around explaining ourselves for the better part of an hour before a detective arrived. Just my luck, it happened to be Detective Warner and his partner Caruso. Warner smiled as he walked through the open front door. He had choppy blond hair and pale gray eyes that would have been *almost* attractive if he wasn't such a tool. "Mr. Sun," he looked past me at Dean, "and Mr. Prescott. Why am I not surprised to see you two here?"

"Because it's our job?" I mumbled, already tired of his abrasive personality.

"*What?*"

"I said, because we just love getting to see you, Warner. You too, Caruso."

Caruso rolled his eyes. Warner didn't even blink. "Who's the deceased?"

I explained the case and how we came to find Caroline. Warner walked further into the living room and noticed the spilled sleeping pills on the floor. "So, suicide, huh?"

"*No,*" Dean stressed. "Caroline wouldn't have killed herself. It must have been an accident."

Warner looked up and smiled. "Sure."

"Let's let the actual professionals tell us, huh?" I suggested. The forensics team was already outside with the body. They'd taken photos and then pulled her out of the water.

"What the hell is going on here?" a loud, booming voice called from behind us.

I turned to find Robert Hydecker standing in the threshold to the living room, his hands on his hips and his face pinched with annoyance. He looked around the room and then his face fell when he spotted Dean. "Dean?" What are you doing here? What's going on?"

Even if he *was* a cheating bastard, his wife had just died.

Warner, not known for his subtlety, said, "Are you the husband?"

Robert turned to look back at the police detectives. "Yes, who are you?"

"I'm Detective Warner. I'm sorry, Mr. Foil, but your wife had a bit of an accident."

"It's Hydecker, not Foil. Caroline wanted to keep her family name, for the company. What kind of accident?" He strode across the living room and must have spotted the body through the large wall of windows out the back. "Oh my God!" He raced through the doors and across the patio.

"Somebody stop him!" Warner shouted. A uniformed officer managed to hold him back before he reached Caroline's body at the edge of the pool.

"What are you doing to her?" he shouted. "What happened?"

Dean held up his hand. "I've got this." He managed to hold his composure as he walked out to Robert, who was now sobbing and sitting on the ground. "Robert?" Robert looked up through his cries. "I'm sorry for your loss."

"What happened?" he repeated, quieter and more controlled this time.

"We don't know," Dean said. "Right now it looks like she might have accidentally passed out while she was sitting here by the pool and fallen in."

"But...why are *you* here?" Robert asked.

Dean hesitated.

There was no sugar coating it. I walked up and introduced myself and explained the situation, being as *delicate* as I could manage. "Your wife hired us to look into something. We were supposed to meet here at the house this morning, and that's when we found her in the pool."

"Hired you?"

"Yes," Dean said. "I work at a detective agency now."

The information seemed to be all too much and Robert fell into another round of sobs.

* * *

Once the police were done with us, I drove Dean home. I parked the car in front of his apartment and turned off the engine. "Are you going to be okay?" I asked. Dean had been distant since he'd seen the body, but he was pretending everything was normal.

He smiled. "Yeah, I'll be fine." He paused. "I guess the case is closed now, since we don't have a client?"

I shrugged. "I would say that's true. Not to be grim, but I don't think Robert will be paying us from her estate once he knows what she hired us for."

"*Hmm.*"

I grabbed Dean's hand across the center console and squeezed. "I'm sorry, Dean."

He took a second and then looked up at me. "I know. Thanks, Noah." He pulled away and opened the door to get out. "I'll see you in the morning."

I shook my head. "You don't have to come in tomorrow if you don't want to."

He bit his lip. "I want to."

"Okay."

"See you then." He closed the door and I watched as he slipped into his apartment building.

I'd seen a lot of disturbing, awful things in my time as a detective, but I'd never had to find the body of a friend. I couldn't imagine how that felt. Our first real case in two weeks and it was already circling the drain. Let's just hope that tomorrow things would change. They had to.

FOUR

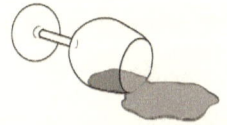

It was nine in the morning when Dean walked into the office the next day. Lexi was at school—for once—and I was sitting in my office looking over the books for the tenth time, hoping to find some money somewhere. Dean smiled as he came into the room, two coffees in hand. He placed one on the desk in front of me. "Extra strong, extra black," he said.

"Thanks." Shouldn't *I* have been the one doing a nice thing for *him*? It was *his* friend that had died, after all.

He took a sip from his own supersized iced cold brew and sat down across from me. The scene mirrored when Dean had first come to me as a client less than three weeks ago. How different my life had become after that day.

"So how does it look?" Dean asked, gesturing to the stack of bills and unpaid client invoices.

I smiled. "Grim."

"Ah." He reached out for my cup. "Maybe I can get a refund on the coffee."

I snatched the cup away from him. "Don't you dare. No take backs."

He laughed. "I was just kidding."

I set down the papers and took a long pull from the warm elixir. "I need it today, more than ever."

Dean paused, looking down at his lap. "Any news on Caroline?"

I shook my head. "I haven't heard anything, and I doubt Warner is going to keep us informed."

Dean let out a deep breath. "I just can't believe that it was an accident, and I *really* can't believe that Caroline would take her own life. She wasn't that type of person."

"I don't know, Dean, people constantly surprise me. As soon as you think you have them all figured out they throw a curveball at you."

He drummed his fingers against the armrest. "I guess so."

"Hello?" a voice from the other room called.

I stood up and walked through the open doorway to the outer office. "Hi?"

A tall, slender woman with curly brown hair stood in the middle of the room. Her eyes were red and her face was puffy—telltale signs that she'd been crying recently, although her cheeks were dry.

"Are you Detective Sun?" she asked.

I nodded. "Yes, how can I help you?"

She reached into her bag and pulled out a business card. "My name is Heather Lawson. I am—or I was—Caroline Foil's personal assistant."

"Oh." I took the card from her outstretched hand. "I'm sorry for your loss. What can I do for you?"

Dean had stood up and was leaning against the doorframe to my office.

"I want to hire you," she said firmly, her brows knit with determination.

"You do?" I asked. "What for?"

She let out a breath. "I want you to prove that Caroline was murdered."

* * *

I ushered her into my office and Dean moved to sit in Lexi's usual spot beside me behind the large wooden desk. "So, Ms. Lawson, what makes you think that Caroline was murdered?" I asked. "The police are convinced that it was an accident."

I didn't tell her that Dean had some of the same suspicions. I wanted to hear *her* reasons.

"Several things." She sat down across from us and pulled a small notebook from her bag. It was bound in black leather and looked expensive.

She turned to a marked page and looked up at us. "The first thing that was totally odd to me was the fact that her dog, Wubby, was locked in the study upstairs."

"That was unusual?" I asked.

She nodded. "Definitely. Caroline lived for that dog. They were codependent. She treated Wubby better than most humans. There's no way that she would lock him in a room and not let him run around freely. She wouldn't do that."

I'd been suspicious yesterday, but I clearly hadn't known Caroline as well as Heather. They must have spent a lot of time together. "Okay, what else were you thinking?" I asked.

She read down her list. "Another big problem is the pills."

"The pills?" Dean asked.

She nodded and pressed her lips together. "Yes, it's true that Caroline religiously took sleeping pills, so it wouldn't be strange that she took some that night. But that bottle they found? Was the wrong brand. Caroline was *very* specific about what she took. I would know, I was the one who purchased her sleeping pills when she forgot to pick some up. She would have never bought that cheap, generic brand."

Interesting. So either she randomly chose to buy a different brand that day, or someone else had brought her the pills. Someone other than Heather.

"Okay." I nudged Dean and he started writing down her observations in the notebook on my desk. "What else?"

Heather took in a deep breath and then looked back at us. "I've known Caroline for years. I've been her personal assistant for three, and I've gotten pretty close with her over that time. I wouldn't say we were *friends*, but we spent most days together. I know her favorite food, her allergies, what kind of movies make her cry, what days she had dates with Robert—all the little things that people don't really think about."

I urged her to continue, not really seeing her point. "Meaning?"

"*Meaning*, she wasn't the type to make mistakes," she replied. "She would never take too many sleeping pills by accident and then fall into the pool. It just wouldn't happen. And the idea that she would kill herself is even *more* laughable." She smiled. "Caroline was a bloodhound, a workhorse, a go-getter. She demolished obstacles, she didn't cower in front of them. There is absolutely no way in hell that she would end her life like that. And in such a benign fashion? If she ever decided to kill herself—and as I already said she never would—it would be in a fiery explosion, or some crazy spectacle that the papers would be talking about for years to come. I just don't buy any of this."

I cocked my head to the side. "Huh, you make a compelling argument." She'd repeated a lot of what Dean had mentioned yesterday. It wasn't in Caroline's nature to make mistakes or give up against challenges.

"And one other big thing," she said, searching through her purse.

I nodded. "Yeah?"

"She was being blackmailed."

Dean sat up straighter in his chair. "Blackmailed?"

"Yes." She pulled a stack of papers from her bag and laid them out on the desk. They were all the same kind of pale blue paper. I read the heading at the top of the page—Hydecker Theater Group. Then I read the actual messages.

2 ThoUsaNd oR yoUr SecRet cOmeS OuT

3K or RoBerT KnoWs

50O oR I'lL tEll EveRyoNe

There were more notes—more or less the same with different amounts of money. No doubt, as Caroline paid the blackmailer they got cocky and asked for more each time.

"Tell them what?" I asked, looking up at Heather.

She shook her head. "I don't know. I never found out what it was about. I don't think Caroline wanted me to know about the notes, but of course I did."

"Where were they sent?" Dean asked.

She gestured with her hand. "Lots of places. Sometimes her house, sometimes the office, sometimes even just under her windshield wiper, or shoved in her mailbox."

"Any suspicions on who could have been sending these notes?" I asked. This was a huge development in the case. If Caroline was being blackmailed, that asked a lot of new questions that needed answered.

She shook her head. "It could be a lot of people. But you see why I think Caroline was murdered, right? There's too many little details that don't add up."

I nodded. "Have you shared any of this with the police?" They were in charge of the case now.

She frowned and bit her lip. "Yes, and that detective guy, Warner, doesn't believe me."

"Even about the blackmail?" Dean asked, sounding surprised.

She rolled her eyes. "He said that it's even more reason why Caroline would kill herself. He's calling it a suicide."

Dean shook his head. I had to agree with both of them. From everything that Heather shared, and my own observations, it did look suspicious.

"Does Robert know about the blackmail?" I asked. Why was Heather coming to us and not Robert? Caroline had been *his* wife.

She shook her head. "No. I haven't told him about it yet. I wanted to hear your opinion first and see if you would take the case."

"Of course we'll take the case," Dean said for the both of us.

Normally I would have liked him to consult me before making such a declarative statement, but I agreed. This case needed to be investigated, especially since Caroline had already been our client. She needed to see justice served. Someone killed Caroline Foil, and we were going to find out who.

"You will?" she asked, a ghost of a smile on her lips.

"Yes, we will." I nodded. "Do you have time to answer some questions now? It's best to get the ball rolling. The police are a whole day ahead of us."

She sat up straighter in her seat, pulling her purse into her lap. "Of course."

"I'm assuming you know what Caroline hired us for since you're here," I asked with a raised brow.

She nodded. "Yes. Although, Caroline kept it brief. I only knew that she'd hired you to follow Robert. She had her suspicions that he was cheating on her. I didn't want to tell her that it was more or less an open secret. Everybody knew."

"Who's everybody?" Dean asked.

She shrugged. "Everyone at the theater, some people at the magazine office. Robert wasn't shy about his affair. It was my understanding that the main reason she hired you two was because she needed the legal proof for her divorce lawyer."

I nodded. "Yes, she mentioned something about that during our first meeting." I rolled a pen between my fingers. "Maybe you can tell us a little about Caroline and Robert's relationship?"

She wiped her hands down her skirt. "Sure. Well, they really only had a *business* relationship. I didn't know them back when they first got married years ago, but for as long as I've worked for Caroline they've had a very distant marriage. Caroline always joked that Robert was married to the theater. That was his passion. It was a big point of contention between the two of them."

Dean bobbed his head and gestured with his hand. "Yeah, Caroline helped Robert buy the theater and fund his productions, right?" Caroline had mentioned it briefly before.

Heather nodded. "That's right. She had a lot of money sunk into that theater, actually. From what I understand, it hasn't been turning a profit. Their productions are too expensive, and they don't fill all their seats. Caroline only kept it open to keep Robert happy."

"That bad, huh?" I asked. "How much money were they losing?"

She pressed her lips together. "I don't know, tens of thousands, I imagine. The upkeep of an old theater like that must take a lot of money."

That was a huge motive. The theater was hemorrhaging money, and someone there was blackmailing Caroline about *something* to the tune of thousands of dollars.

"Do you think it's possible that Robert was the one blackmailing Caroline?" I asked, partially to myself, but also to the room. I often thought better aloud.

Heather made a face. "*Hmm*, I don't think he'd need to. Even though the theater wasn't doing well she always kept paying for it. Though recently, on this newest production, she had been pulling the reins a little tighter. You know, having meetings with the staff and explaining budget cuts, etc."

Dean leaned forward. "I'm guessing that didn't go over too well?"

She almost smiled. "No, not at all. That's why I think the blackmailer probably works at the theater. She started getting the notes soon after she told everyone they'd have to scale back their vision."

"That makes sense," I said. "And how did Robert react to the news?"

"I mean," she started, "he wasn't exactly *happy* about it, of course, but he always tried to save face and be positive with his staff. I think most of them see him as sort of the fun uncle who lets them do whatever they want, and they see Caroline as the evil stepmother."

"And what is this new production?" Dean asked.

She rolled her wrist in the air. "Uh, I guess you could say it's sort of a modern interpretation of the suffragette movement, in a similar style to Hamilton? It's called The Marching Cry. "

Dean furrowed his brow. "It's a musical?"

She hummed and shook her head. "Yes, and no. It has music, that's for sure. I don't know if you could call it a *musical*, though."

That was confusing, and also totally not important to the investigation. I tried to get us back on track. "So just for the record, where were *you* Friday night, Heather?" We didn't have an exact time of death yet, unless the police decided to throw us a bone. I'd have to call one of my buddies in forensics and see if he'd divulge.

She flushed. "Oh, right. I didn't think about that, but of course you'd need to know my alibi. I was out with a couple friends that night. We went to a comedy club and had a few drinks. They can vouch for me."

"What time did you get home?" I asked.

She shook her head. "I didn't go home. We stayed out past one o'clock, and then my friend Samantha took me to her house in Pasadena. I slept there."

"Okay, I'll need your friend's name and number, please." I jotted the information down on the notepad. "The last thing I want to talk about is the house," I said.

Heather pinched her brows. "The house?"

I nodded. "Yes, we're trying to figure out if Caroline let her attacker inside, or if they had their own way in. Do you have a key to the house?"

She bobbed her head. "Of course." She rummaged through her purse and pulled out a keychain that held way too many keys—more than half a dozen. She plucked a small silver key and held it up. "Right here."

"Okay, and have you ever given that out to anyone, even just once?" I asked.

She shook her head quickly. "No, of course not. I wouldn't do that."

I smiled. "It's my job to ask. Do you know of anyone else who has a key?"

She pressed her lips together in thought. "*Hmm*, the housekeeper has a key—Matilda—and Robert's assistant, Tim."

"Okay," I wrote that all down for later.

Dean interjected, "I couldn't help but notice that when we were at the house the alarm didn't go off. Someone had deactivated it. Was that unusual?"

She let out a heavy sigh. "Yes, and no. Typically, the alarm would always be armed, but Caroline was having the upstairs bathroom remodeled, and the workers kept tripping the alarms, so she had to turn them off occasionally. It's possible she just forgot to reset it that day."

Hmm. That seemed convenient.

"Okay, that's helpful, thanks," I said. "One last question. Is there anyone you think we should pay close attention to? I know you said that it could have been anyone that was blackmailing her, but can you think of someone specifically that would want to kill Caroline?"

She answered immediately, "Yes, Adeya Nwadike."

"Who's Adeya Nwadike?" I asked.

Dean nudged my shoulder. "You don't know who Adeya is? International fashion critic? She was at the Met Ball last year."

"*Okay.*" I didn't exactly keep up with the fashion world like Dean.

"Yes, that's the one," Heather said. "She wrote some quite nasty things about Caroline in the LA Times after they had a bad interaction at a fashion show. Caroline then sued Adeya for defamation and pulled some strings to get her fired from the Times."

"And you think she wants revenge?" I asked.

She nodded. "Oh I *know* so. Even with the defamation suit going on Adeya posted constantly about Caroline online about how much she hated her. It was a bad year for the magazine."

"Okay, that's a good place to start." I stood up. "Thanks for answering our questions. We should probably talk with Robert soon. Do *you* want to tell him that you hired us, or do you want us to make it a surprise?"

She shook her head quickly. "I'll tell him right after this and set up a meeting for you, hopefully today. He took Caroline's death hard, but I know he's going to throw himself into his work at the theater, it's what he always does."

"Okay, we'll wait for your call, then," I said.

I shook her hand and led her out of the office. When I came back, Dean was smiling at me.

I shook my head and crossed my arms. "What?"

He raised one brow. "I noticed you didn't get her payment information?"

I shrugged. "We'll deal with that later. We have people to talk to. Let's track down this Adeya woman."

"*Right.*"

I rolled my eyes. "Let's get a move on, Dean. I have a feeling this case is going to move quickly."

"Don't they always?"

I flicked his shoulder. "Start googling."

"God, you're so pushy." Dean smiled and started typing on my laptop.

FIVE

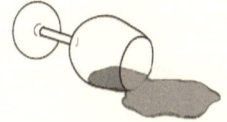

"Shouldn't we be talking to Robert first?" Dean asked as I was writing down the address we'd found for Adeya. It wasn't too far from the office on the east side of Hollywood.

"Why do you say that?" I asked.

He waved his hand. "Well, isn't it the partner like fifty percent of the time?"

I nodded. "Yes, that's true, however we were watching Robert that night while Caroline was being killed in another city an hour away. That's a pretty strong alibi, wouldn't you say?"

"I guess you're right," he mumbled.

"Besides, I thought Robert was your friend?" I said. "Do you want him to be guilty of something?"

Dean scoffed. "I mean he *was* cheating on Caroline, and I wouldn't say we were that close. I was *friends* with Caroline, I was *friendly* with Robert."

"*Hmm.* Why do you think that was?"

He pursed his lips. "I don't know. I mean, Caroline could be closed off sometimes, but we still talked about personal things. I never really got a good read on Robert. He was a very cardboard sort of person. Definitely not the type I would associate with being in the dramatic world of theater production. I just always saw him as Caroline's husband. We played golf together a few times as a group, but I never spent any time alone with him."

That was odd. But I couldn't exactly judge the guy on being quiet and closed off. Those weren't crimes.

"We'll talk to him after we talk to Adeya," I said. "Let's just see what she has to say first. Since according to Heather, she has the best motive for wanting to kill Caroline."

He rolled his shoulders. "Okay, you know more about this whole detective thing than I do."

I nodded and left it at that. Dean had some good instincts, but he was right—he was new, and I'd been doing this for years. Sometimes practice was better than instinct.

We left the office and got in my black nineties Jeep.

The address we'd found on a locator database was for a townhouse in East Hollywood. It was fairly nice, but not mansion-in-the-hills nice. It sat up against twenty identical townhouses along an alleyway. I parked in the alley and we got out.

"So what's the play here?" Dean asked as we walked up to the door.

"*Hmm*, it depends," I said. "Caroline's death hasn't hit the headlines yet, so either Adeya's feeling cocky that she got away with it, or she's nervous that someone is going to find her out. We'll know our strategy in a second."

"I'll be good cop," Dean whispered as I knocked on the door.

"Why am I always bad cop?" I asked with a tinge of annoyance.

He shrugged. "You're more intimidating than me."

I didn't know how to take that, so I said nothing. We waited for a minute or two before the door opened. A skinny blonde woman in her late twenties answered. "Yeah?"

Dean started us off. "Sorry to bother you, we're looking for Adeya Nwadike. Does she still live here?"

The girl rolled her eyes. "No, *thank God*. She was, like, my roommate for a while, but then she stopped paying rent, so I kicked her ass out."

"Oh," Dean raised his eyebrows. "Do you happen to know where she lives now?"

The girl scoffed. "No, and I don't *want* to know. That woman is crazy."

Crazy enough to kill?

"Okay, thanks for the information," I said and turned away before she could close the door on us.

"Well I guess just finding an address online isn't as simple as it looks," Dean said under his breath.

I laughed through my nose. "It never is, is it? Time for plan B."

"What's plan B?"

I glanced over at him and raised an eyebrow. "You know what plan B is."

* * *

"Sure, I can find her," Lexi said over the phone. I had her on speaker so Dean could hear.

She was at home for the weekend. Her dad—my brother Mark—was still hounding her about her grades, so Lexi hadn't been helping us out at the office as much lately. Not that we'd had any important cases that needed attention the last two weeks.

"That would be great," I said. "She's our number one suspect right now."

Dean pinched his brows. "I mean, we just started like thirty minutes ago, but yeah."

Lexi laughed. "Are you keeping my uncle out of trouble, Dean?"

Dean frowned. "Of course not."

"*Good*," she said. "Uncle Noah needs some trouble now and again." She shuffled something around. "Just give me a few minutes. I need to deep dive."

"Okay." I gave Dean an admonishing look. "I'll call back in ten minutes."

"Cool, bye."

"Bye." I hung up the phone and leaned back in the car seat. It was a hot, sunny spring day in Los Angeles and I had the top down on the Jeep. It wasn't good for the leather, but the air conditioner rarely worked, and having the breeze felt like ambrosia. Even with just a thin t-shirt, the material was already sticking to my skin.

"Do you really think it's Adeya? We don't know anything about her," Dean pointed out.

"We know that Caroline got her fired," I said. "That creates a lot of resentment. Remember what I told you, Dean—motives fall under three categories: opportunity, revenge, and gain. Now, most of the time murder falls under gain because people are greedy and want what others have, or they're gaining power as opposed to money. The second most common is revenge. Or a combination of the two."

"I know, the details just don't make sense to me."

"How so?" I asked.

He threw his arm over the back of the seat and leaned toward me. "Well, if this was a murder of revenge how would Adeya have gotten in the house? Caroline certainly wouldn't have let her inside."

"We'll ask her when we see her."

He went on, "And what about the wine? Caroline obviously didn't open a bottle for her worst enemy to drink with her by the fire."

I let out a breath. "I understand what you're saying, Dean, but this is where Heather thinks we should look first. She might not be correct, but Heather has known Caroline for years—they saw each other every day. Her opinion matters here."

"*Hmm*, I suppose you're right."

"Thank you."

A silence stretched between us. I was painfully aware of how close Dean was to me. How was he not dying of heat in that suit? I was already flushed, the back of my neck warm.

"Well, what about Heather herself?" Dean asked, pulling me from my thoughts.

"For the murder?" I asked. He nodded. "That would be strange since she's the one who hired us. I'm not saying it's impossible. You see that every once in a while—a killer who wants to be a part of the investigation, help the cops. It's one in a thousand, though. Heather doesn't strike me as the type."

"She did have access to the house and intimate knowledge of Caroline's schedule slash daily routine," Dean argued.

"But what's the motive?" I asked. "The only thing I see right now is that Heather is out of a job. I doubt Caroline left her any money, and it seemed like they had a pretty good relationship from what we've heard so far."

He slouched and tapped his fingers on the side of the door. "She seems sweet, but maybe she's hiding something? Maybe she harbored some resentment against Caroline, maybe she was in love with Robert?"

I waved my hand. "Let's not get caught up in the *what if* game, we just started the investigation. We don't have enough evidence to support *anything* yet."

"I guess you're right."

There was a pause in conversation. It was starting to get hot outside, although luckily the alley was mostly shaded.

"Do you want to get dinner later?" Dean asked out of the blue.

My brain took a minute to catch up. "Wait, what?" I pinched my brows together. "What do you mean?"

He shrugged his shoulders and gazed at the houses lined up along the alley. "Exactly what I just said—do you want to get dinner later?"

He'd said it so casually, but I could feel the undertone hiding below the surface. "I have plans," I lied.

He knit his brows and looked me in the face. "No you don't."

I met his gaze. "Yes I do. What do you mean, *no I don't?*"

"Because I know you, Noah." He laughed. "You don't have plans because you *never* have plans. Feeding Captain doesn't count as *plans*."

The mention of my dog as my only companion stung. "I know what you're asking, Dean, and I told you that we couldn't go there," I said sternly. "We are working professionals. You're my employee, nothing more."

He pursed his lips. "I was just asking if you wanted to get some food, is that a crime?"

I narrowed my eyes. "You *know* what you were asking."

He let out a dramatic sigh and slung his arm out the open window. "Fine, you caught me, detective. I was asking you on a date. Why won't you accept my offer?" He grinned with what I imagined he thought was unrefusable charm.

"You know why. I just told you—it would be unprofessional," I stated plainly, not giving the conversation more emotion than necessary.

He raised an eyebrow. "But that's the *only* reason, right? It's not because you don't *want* to, it's because you think you shouldn't."

I sputtered to speak, and my neck flushed. "I don't know what you want from me, Dean."

He smiled, staring me down. "To have dinner, *obviously*."

I was saved from answering when Lexi called me back. I picked up the phone quickly. "Yeah?" I glanced at Dean. He shook his head and smirked.

"I found her," she said.

"You did?"

"It wasn't easy," Lexi said. "She's really hidden herself online."

I put the call on speaker phone. "How'd you do it?"

"She tagged a friend in a photo on social media, and that friend later took pictures with Adeya in front of a house in Glendale. Now, the house isn't Adeya's, but it just so happens to be her sister's. I was able to call her sister, and I told her I was Caroline's assistant Heather, and that I had some important information to send Adeya. Then the sister gave me Adeya's new address. It's in Burbank."

"Wow, that's impressive." Lexi was the smartest sixteen-year-old I knew. She was definitely wasting her talents on high school.

Lexi laughed. "Thanks. I'm sending you the address now."

I couldn't believe her sister just gave Lexi Adeya's address without verifying who she was. "This is great, thanks for the help. I hope you're not too bored at home right now."

Lexi sighed. "Dad has me doing some extra college interview prep with a coach who apparently gets a lot of kids into ivy leagues. Grandma found him."

"How's that going?" Dean asked.

She groaned in response.

I chuckled. "That good, huh?"

"Yeah, hopefully I'll be un-grounded soon and I can help you guys more. Keep me updated in the case document."

"Will do, thanks again."

"Bye, Uncle Noah. Bye, Dean.

"Bye."

I hung up the phone and put the new address into the navigation app. The house wasn't too far away.

I was glad for the distraction as I pulled the car back onto the road. It wasn't that I didn't like Dean. I did, obviously. I'd kissed him almost two weeks ago. But it had been a mistake. Even if Dean really did like me —which even though he kept asking me on dates, I was hard pressed to believe he was being genuine—everything was a game to him, even people. People were things to dissect and figure out.

How could I tell if he was being truthful? And even if he *was* being truthful, I'd had such a bad experience dating my ex-business partner Malcolm that I was hesitant to ever get myself into that situation again. Business and pleasure didn't mix well. It was better to keep the two separate. And now that Dean was working for me to make some honest income, he couldn't be considered just a friend or a client anymore.

I glanced over at Dean and he smiled carefree. He probably wasn't overthinking the situation like I was. This was all a fun game to him. I let out a held breath.

When we reached the house I was surprised to find it was large and in an expensive neighborhood. Definitely not what I'd been expecting since Adeya was supposed to be down on her luck after getting fired from the newspaper.

Dean looked up at the towering facade. "Wow, where'd she get the money?"

"Exactly what I was thinking," I said.

Dean hopped out of the car. "Do you think she could be the one who was blackmailing Caroline?"

"*Hmm*, I don't think so. Besides the fact that the blackmail notes were on theater letterhead, I don't think a couple thousand dollars here and there would support this lifestyle. This is bigger than that."

He shrugged. "Maybe you're right. Let's go find out."

We walked up the drive to the front porch and knocked on the door. After a minute or two a woman answered. She had deep brown skin, hair in long braids, and was wearing a yellow sundress like she was about to go out on a picnic at the park. "Yes?" she asked.

Dean smiled. "Are you Adeya Nwadike?"

She arched a brow and took a step back. "Who's asking?"

"We're from The Golden Sun Detective Agency," I said. "We're looking into the death of Caroline Foil. It's our understanding that you knew Caroline." I decided to go straight for the jugular. After all, I was *bad cop*.

She opened her mouth and then closed it again. "Caroline is dead?"

She was trying to mask her shock, but it was pretty obvious to me that this was the first time she was hearing about Caroline's death.

"Yes, murdered," I said.

"Murdered?" The color drained from her face, and her eyebrows rose.

Dean continued where I left off. "We were told by her assistant that you knew Caroline?"

After a long pause she nodded. "Uh, yes. I suppose you could say that."

"How well did you know her?" I asked. I was playing dumb to see if I could get any extra information out of her. I didn't need to reveal my whole hand right off the bat.

She seemed to sober up a bit and scoffed. "That bitch got me fired."

Whoa, attitude change.

She placed a hand on her hip and steeled her features, no longer caught off guard.

"Right, and why exactly did she get you fired?" Dean asked, chipper and sweet as syrup. "Her assistant wasn't too clear on that."

She looked between the two of us, putting things together. "How did you find me?"

Dean shrugged. "Your sister gave us your address."

She clucked her tongue and said under her breath, "Girl, why would you tell people my business?" She sighed and turned her attention back to us. "It's not exactly a secret. It was all over the internet."

"We don't surf the web much," I said deadpan.

"Whatever." She frowned. "I called Caroline out for using fur in her latest Fall quarter issue of Runway, and how she was a hypocrite since she donated to a handful of animal charities with her family's legacy funds. She didn't like that. She had The Times retract the article, and she convinced them to fire me. Then she had the nerve to *sue me* for defamation." She laughed. "Which she *lost*. You can't defame someone if the information is true. She went crazy. She called up everywhere that I'd interviewed at and told them if they hired me she'd badmouth them to their corporate sponsors." She shook her head. "She loved that silly little dog of hers *so* much, but yet she still promoted fur in her magazine that's read by millions of people. It was disgusting."

"So you had a pretty contentious relationship?" I asked.

Adeya pursed her lips. "You could say that. I hated that bitch."

"Enough to want her dead?" I added.

She rolled her eyes. "You can't be serious."

Dean leaned in and whispered, "He's serious."

"No, I didn't kill her." She scoffed. "Let me tell you guys something —when you truly hate someone, you go out of your way to never think about them, never see them, never spend a second of your mental energy on them ever again. I moved on months ago."

"We can see that." I gestured to the house. "Clearly *someone* hired you."

She nodded. "I hired *myself.*" She lowered her voice even though there was no one around to overhear her. "I started a fashion news account anonymously and used that hypocrite as my first article. It went viral overnight. Suddenly *I* was the one getting corporate sponsors and ad dollars. So no, I don't ever think about Caroline, and I certainly didn't care enough about her to kill her. Though I can't say I'm sad she's dead."

Harsh.

"Just out of curiosity," Dean started. "Can you tell us where you were Friday night?"

She frowned, having clearly moved past the whole *murder* thing. "I was in New York following a story." She pulled out her phone and clicked on something. "Here, I still have the ticket on my phone." She showed us the digital ticket, and the dates checked out. She was in New York until late last night. There was no way she could have been in LA killing Caroline at the same time.

"Okay, thanks," I mumbled. Dean had been right. Adeya was too obvious, it didn't fit.

"One more question, Dean said. "If you had to guess, who do you think could have killed her?"

Adeya shrugged and crossed her arms. "Her husband probably."

Dean raised a brow. "Why do you say that?"

"Because the tabloids have been rumoring their divorce for years. It was obvious how much they hated each other."

"*Huh*," he said.

I smiled. "If we have any more questions we'll contact you."

She scoffed. "Well *don't*. I refuse to have anything to do with that woman ever again. I wish you luck, but lose my number." She moved away to shut the door. "And I'm going to kill my stupid sister."

Dean turned to me and grinned. "See?"

I shook my head. "Just because you might have been right doesn't mean you could have known that without interviewing her first," I pointed out.

"What do you mean, *might have*? She clearly didn't do it, she has the perfect alibi."

I pursed my lips and shrugged. "Maybe *too* perfect."

He laughed through his nose and rolled his eyes. "What, you think she faked a plane ticket?"

I put my hands in my pockets and started walking back toward the Jeep. "I'm just saying we need to confirm and call the airline, that's all."

He chuckled and jogged to catch up to me. "You're unbelievable."

"Thanks."

As soon as we got in the car my phone buzzed with a text.

H: I told Robert about hiring you. He's all for it, and he's offered to take over the cost. You can talk to him any time today. Here's the address for the theater.

The address was in Hollywood, of course. I couldn't imagine how much money Caroline was paying to rent a place like that in the middle of Hollywood. It must have been a fortune. No wonder they'd fought about it all the time.

"We have the address for the theater," I said.

Dean grinned. "Good, let's go talk to our killer."

I rolled my eyes. "You watch too much TV, Dean. It's not always the husband. Especially when he has an ironclad alibi."

Dean pressed his lips together. "That might all be true, but I could *still* be right."

"Sure, *anything is possible*," I said sarcastically. I started the engine and drove back toward Hollywood.

SIX

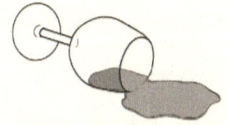

The Hydecker Theater was located in the middle of Hollywood, tucked in along a row of other businesses. I had to pay for street parking around the block in order to get a spot. The tourists were busy wandering the streets, enjoying the warm Los Angeles spring sunshine.

"Question," Dean said as we slipped out of the car and walked up the block.

"Answer," I replied dryly.

"Ha, ha." He narrowed his eyes. "So why do you think someone was dumb enough to write their blackmail note on theater letterhead? Isn't the whole point of blackmail to be anonymous? Why draw attention to yourself like that?"

I cocked my head to the side. "*Eh,* that honestly doesn't tell us much. It tells us the same thing it did to Caroline—the blackmailer is probably someone at the theater."

"Why do you say *probably*?"

We passed a cart vendor selling signed movie posters—all fakes—and a semi-passable Superman cosplayer taking photos with an Asian tourist.

"Because they might have used that letterhead on purpose to throw Caroline off the scent," I explained. "It might have been someone *outside* the theater, like Robert, or maybe his assistant Tim."

"Or Heather?" he asked.

I pressed my lips together. "Possibly, but I don't see what motive she has. She seemed pretty genuine when we talked with her."

He nodded. "Yeah, I kinda agree. She's too sweet, and she's not faking it, trust me."

"Dealt with a lot of *fake* people?" I asked with an arched brow.

He rolled his eyes at the dig and caught up to my fast walking pace. "Shut up, you know what I meant. I've talked with a lot of people in LA that want a lot of things. Everybody has some kind of agenda here. Heather seemed real."

I nodded. I agreed with him for the most part. Heather didn't seem the type to murder *or* to blackmail. It *would* be a diabolical twist to hire a private detective to investigate her own crimes, though. Unlikely as it was.

The Hydecker theater was built in the 1930s with Roman columns on either side of the facade and an iconic glass ticket booth that had faded out of fashion. Many of the historic theaters had been going bankrupt in the last decade. No wonder Caroline was trying to cut back on the theater's budget.

There was a large poster for the new production that was premiering in a couple weeks—The Marching Cry. Three women in Edwardian dress were holding protest signs in each hand, white sashes across their frames.

We tried the front doors, but of course they were locked. It was the middle of the morning, and there was no matinee today. "Around back," I said, but Dean was already walking ahead of me. The alley wasn't nearly as pretty as the facade with its beige painted brick. We turned the corner past an open chain-link gate to the back of the building.

"Bingo," Dean said with a smile. A metal door painted the same color as the rest of the building was wide open, and the air was still heavy with the scent of cigarette smoke. We wandered inside and were met with a long hallway with half a dozen doors on either side—some open, some closed.

It didn't take long for someone to spot us. A woman wearing black yoga pants and a black t-shirt holding a clipboard had her eyes narrowed on us. "Can I help you two?"

She probably thought we were toxic fans or merch sellers looking for autographs from the actors. "We have an appointment to talk with Mr. Hydecker," I said. "Can you point us in the direction of his office?"

"Oh." She visibly relaxed. "Yeah, it's up the spiral stairs and to the right, you can't miss it." She pointed to the staircase at the end of the hallway.

"Thanks, and who are you?" I asked.

"I'm Gwen Flakk, the stage manager." She pushed her short bob of blonde hair behind her ear. "And you guys are..."

"Private detectives," Dean supplied.

She crossed her arms and rocked on her heels. "Oh. I heard about Caroline. Awful thing. Is that what you're here about?"

I nodded. "Yes, Mr. Hydecker has hired us to look into his wife's death. Anyway, thanks for the help. We might want to speak to you later. Will you be around?"

She shrugged. "I'm always around. I practically live here."

It was hard to get a good read on her. I couldn't tell if she was just being polite or if she was genuinely sad that Caroline had died.

"Okay, we'll find you after." We passed her toward the stairs and climbed them to the second story.

To the right was an open-air catwalk where you could see the back set of curtains down below. The offices must have been right behind the stage. That would have to be loud during productions. I wondered how they got any work done with all the noise. There were two offices that sat across from each other at the end of the catwalk. Only one of the doors was open. I knocked on the doorframe and Robert looked up. "Hello, Mr. Hydecker. Heather told you we were coming?" I asked hopefully.

He nodded and gestured for us to come in. "Yes, she did. Please, sit down."

There were two upholstered office chairs in front of his desk. The room was small and sparsely furnished with a skinny bookshelf filled with books and records. The desk sat on the right side of the room across from a large window that looked out to the back of the stage. Could you watch productions from up here? The desk was messy, piled with papers and objects.

We sat down. Robert was fidgeting with his cuffs and wiping his hands on his trousers.

"How are you doing, Robert?" Dean asked.

Robert shook his head. "You know, as well as I can, I guess. I thought about staying home, but who can hang around in a place where their wife died? I'm living at the Carlton right now." He sighed and pulled a hand through his salt and pepper hair. "On top of that, our new production is supposed to debut in two weeks, and nothing is ready. The police are hounding me about Caroline, and now Heather thinks it was murder."

"And what do *you* think?" I asked. I watched him closely as he answered, looking for ticks and tells.

"Well, she made a compelling argument." He clasped his hands together on top of the desk. "Caroline was very type A, very exact. So all those small details that the cops are willing to look past must be important. I just can't believe that Caroline would make such a stupid mistake, and there's absolutely no way she would ever kill herself, even if..." He went silent, his eyes widening.

"She knew that you'd been cheating on her?" Dean supplied.

He nodded. "Yes, that." He furrowed his brow. "How did you know about that? Did Caroline tell you?"

Now came the awkward part. "Caroline hired us to follow you and acquire proof of the affair," I said simply. Better to pull off the bandage quickly rather than draw it out.

He gaped. "What? Why would she do that?" His face drained of color.

I was a little surprised. With how obvious the affair was to Heather and others in Caroline's life, I found it hard to believe that Robert would be shocked she'd known the truth.

Dean answered, "She was going to divorce you, and she wanted physical evidence for her lawyer."

Robert let out a deep breath. "*Oh Caroline.*" He gazed down at the desk and then back up to us. "So I guess you two know about me and Cami?"

I nodded. "A little. Why don't you tell us some more? Did you meet here at the theater?"

He hesitated and then waved his hand through the air. "Why does it matter? Do you think someone killed Caroline because of my affair?"

Dean shook his head. "No, probably not, but background information could help us uncover something that was missed."

"*Hmm.*" He shifted in his high-backed leather desk chair. "Yes, I met Cami here at the theater. She's the lead in our newest production, as I'm sure you already know."

"And how long have you two been seeing each other?" I asked.

He shook his head. "A few months, give or take. I knew Cami before we cast the new production." He lowered his voice even though there was no one around to hear him. "I don't want this getting out to the press, or even the rest of the theater. I don't want people thinking I gave her the lead role because I was seeing her. Camilla is *very* talented, and that is the only reason I cast her as our lead."

I was sure that was the *only* reason. Though, I couldn't truly judge if she was talented or not. I wasn't really an appreciator of the arts like Dean.

"Right, she was amazing in The Scarlet Letter," Dean said, making my point.

Robert nodded. "Exactly. You understand, then."

"So you're saying that no one else at the theater knew about your relationship with Camilla?" I asked, already knowing it wasn't the truth. People talked, and if Caroline had figured it out, I was sure that others had as well. Heather said as much.

"Only my assistant, Tim Grant," Robert said. "He booked accommodations for us often."

"Like the one to Newport Beach?" Dean asked.

He nodded slowly. "So you two were...there?"

Dean grinned. "Yes, nice car by the way."

"Obviously, we don't think you or Camilla had any involvement in your wife's death." I threw that out there just to see his reaction.

He frowned and pinched his eyebrows. "*Obviously?* Are you trying to imply that someone *else* thinks I killed my wife? I loved Caroline."

Dean made a noise he, no doubt, tried to suppress, and I sent him a nasty look. Don't give your suspects anything to use against you during an interview. Dean would have to learn that the hard way.

"*What?*" Robert asked tersely.

Dean shrugged. "Nothing, just that you obviously didn't love Caroline enough to be faithful, that's all."

Now he'd done it. Robert flushed and scooted back from his chair. "If that's all you need, you can move on to other avenues." He stood. "I don't want you talking to Camilla. She had no part in whatever happened to Caroline, and there's no sense in upsetting her. If I find out that you've interviewed her like some common criminal I'll be *very* upset."

I smiled, trying to ease the tension in the room. "Of course, Mr. Hydecker. You're the client, we follow *your* lead."

Dean looked like he wanted to say something, but I placed a warning hand on his shoulder and urged him out the door. "We'll let you know when we have some information to share or if we have any more questions."

Robert nodded. "Fine."

I shut the door behind us and glared at Dean. "Don't do that again."

He smiled, all innocent boyish charm. "Do what?"

"You *know* what. Don't rile up a suspect unless it's a tactic to get them to reveal information."

He frowned. "How do you know I wasn't using a tactic?"

I crossed my arms and stared him down. "*You weren't.*"

He rolled his eyes and turned away. "Whatever, who are we talking to next?"

I looked across the catwalk at the second office. The door was closed, but through the window I spotted a thin pale man in his late twenties or early thirties who was hunched over the desk sipping on a coffee. He was wearing a poorly fitted suit that would make Dean cringe, and his mousy brown hair was tousled and unkempt.

I was about to walk over when I got a text. I read it quickly and said, "My guy in forensics says the medical examiner placed Caroline's death between eleven and midnight."

Dean nodded. "Okay, so we can get more specific with our timeline now."

"Exactly. Let's talk to the assistant." I knocked on the closed office door and cracked it open. "Are you Mr. Hydecker's assistant? Tim Grant?" I asked, though I was almost sure I was correct.

He startled at the two of us standing in the doorway. "*What?* Oh, yes. Hello?"

"Can we come in?" I asked. "I'm Detective Sun, and this is my associate Mr. Prescott. We've been hired by Mr. Hydecker to look into the suspicious circumstances surrounding his wife's death."

He adjusted his thin, wire frame glasses. "Oh yes." He shook his head. "I can't believe it." He gestured for us to enter. "Come in, please."

This room was not half as nice as Robert's office and was clearly not Tim's permanent space. Posters for old productions hung on the walls, and the room smelled like stale cigarettes from years of abuse. Tim didn't seem like a smoker, though he had an almost sickly constitution about him.

We sat down in two—much less comfortable—folding chairs and got to business. "We just finished talking with Mr. Hydecker about where he was on Friday night. He told us you booked him those reservations?" I asked.

Tim nodded, fidgeting with his fingers on top of the desk. "I do everything for Robert. He's not very handy when it comes to little details like that."

Hmm, another strike against someone who is supposed to run a theater.

"So, you did a lot for Robert," I said. "Do you have access to the house? Do you have your own key?"

He nodded. "Yes, I'm at the house almost every day. Robert likes updates made in person rather than on the phone. He says he likes using the drive back and forth to talk things through and get work done."

"*Hmm,* so far there's you, Heather—Robert of course—and Caroline who all had a key to the house. Am I missing anyone?"

"Well the cleaners had their own key," Tim pointed out.

"Yes, Heather told us that," I said.

He added, "And of course the spare."

"The spare?" Dean asked.

That was the first we'd heard of a spare key.

Tim bobbed his head. "Robert always kept a spare at the theater in case of emergencies. Sometimes he'd leave something in his home office, and when I wasn't around he'd send Gwen or Harrison to go pick up some papers, or his laptop, or something like that from the house."

"And where is that key now?" I asked.

Tim pinched his brows. "It should be around here somewhere." He opened the desk drawer and started rummaging through it.

I glanced at Dean. This case was getting messier and messier. Apparently *everyone* had access to their multi-million dollar mansion and *everyone* knew the gate code.

"I uh—I can't seem to find it," Tim said after a minute of frantic searching.

Dean said what I was thinking, "Well that's not good."

Tim furrowed his brow and pressed his lips together into a flat line. "It probably just got misplaced. Or maybe one of the staff members has it and just forgot to put it back. That's possible, right?"

"Right." It's also possible that since everyone at the theater knew about this lucky spare key our killer took it when no one was around and used it to break into Caroline's house and then kill her. "So where were *you* Friday night, Mr. Grant?" I asked. Tim reminded me of one of those little shaky white dogs. He wasn't intimidating in the slightest, but looks could be deceiving.

He looked up with wide, pale blue eyes. "Me?"

"Yes, you."

"Uh," he shook his head and wracked his brain, "I was at my parents' house for dinner."

"All night?" Dean clarified.

He nodded. "Yes, my parents live in the desert, so I slept over and drove back in the morning."

"So if we called your parents right now they'd corroborate your story?" I asked.

"What do you mean?" His eyebrows shot up. "Of course they would."

Because no one's parents have ever lied for them before.

"*Okay*," I said. "So you weren't anywhere near the house at the time of the murder?"

He looked between the two of us quickly. "*Murder?*"

Dean almost laughed. "What did you think we were talking about?"

"I thought Caroline's death was suspicious because of the pills," he said, shaking his head softly. "You're saying you think someone *killed* her?"

Wow, Tim was *clearly* slow on the uptake. "Yes, Mr. Grant, that is what we're saying."

He leaned back and cleared his throat. "Oh God. That's awful."

He truly seemed shocked that someone would want to murder Caroline. It was a curious reaction.

"Having been Robert's assistant for a long time, is there anyone you can think of that might have wanted to hurt his wife?" I asked.

After a moment he looked up from the desk and shook his head. "No, I mean...everybody liked Caroline."

That was the total opposite of what Heather had told us. Was he just dumb, or did he truly believe that?

"So you have no ideas for us?" Dean pressed.

He conceded with a half-hearted shrug. "Well, she did have a bit of an argument with Harrison, the lighting director."

Dean arched a brow. "An argument?"

He nodded. "I don't remember what it was about exactly, but I could hear it from all the way up on the catwalk, so clearly they got loud."

"Okay, thanks." I wrote that down on my notepad to ask about again later. "Anything else you can think of?"

He took a moment to think and then shook his head. "I don't know. I didn't see Caroline that often, really. She stopped by about once a week to see how the production was going and to make any financial suggestions, but other than that I hardly knew her. I was Robert's assistant, not hers."

"I understand." I stood up, and Dean followed my lead. "Well, thanks for your time, if we have any more questions we'll call you."

He bobbed his head. "I'm sorry I couldn't be more help." He reached out and shook both our hands."

Dean closed the door and walked a few paces away before saying, "He's hiding something."

I crossed my arms. "Why do you say that?"

Dean frowned. "I don't know. There was something about his body language. Every time you asked him a question he almost sighed with relief, like he was anticipating something he didn't want you to ask."

"*Hmm*, you got all that from such a short conversation?" I could tell Tim was fidgety and nervous, but I didn't notice about the questions. I was more focused on his answers.

Dean nodded. "We should definitely talk to him again, maybe when he least expects it."

"Okay, good thinking." I jotted that down. "It was strange that he claimed to barely know Caroline. I mean, he went to their house almost every day for years. Surely he saw her at least a little bit."

"I agree," Dean said. "He was trying too hard to distance himself from her. Maybe he was just nervous? I don't know."

"Well whatever the reason, we have a lot more people to talk to, and hopefully they're all here today."

"Do you want to talk to Harrison next?" Dean asked.

I shook my head. "Let's leave him for last. I want to get a sense of who he is from his co-workers. You know, you can get a totally different perspective from someone's peers rather than their boss."

Dean straightened his tie. "Of course."

As we reached the end of the hall, Tim stepped out of his office and slipped into Robert's across the walkway. Whatever he had to say, it was loud. I could hear the deep base of Robert's voice all the way at the other end of the catwalk.

"Someone's not happy," Dean said.

I shook my head. "No indeed."

SEVEN

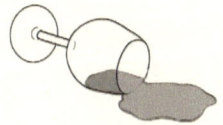

"Let's go find that stage manager—Gwen," Dean said. "If anyone knows some dirt, it's gonna be the stage manager."

"Why do you say that?" I asked. I wasn't completely sure what a stage manager actually did. I was guessing she managed...the stage?

"Because the stage manager is one step below the director. They're in charge of figuring out everything the director wants. It's like production in Hollywood. They get the real shit done. She probably knows every single person here."

Maybe that was why Gwen had looked so stressed out earlier. Robert had likely been passing off all the difficult tasks onto her.

I nodded. It was annoying being around someone who knew more about something than I did. "Um, okay, let's do that, I guess." I was used to calling the shots, so it was hard to let Dean take the wheel. Especially when he was probably right. I was out of my depths, but I didn't dare tell him that. He'd just grin and rub my face in it.

We went downstairs and found Gwen standing in a small booth backstage. It must have been what passed as her office. It was painted the same matte black as the rest of the stage and surrounding areas. The booth had a short counter stacked with papers and clipboards. The walls of the booth were covered in painted signatures and worn-from-age posters.

"Ah, you're back. Did you find him?" she asked, barely sparing us a glance. She was looking down at a pile of papers which had lines of notes in red ink all over the margins.

"Yes, thanks." Dean smiled his playboy grin. "We actually wanted to talk to *you* for a minute, if you have time?"

She sighed and placed her hand on her hip. "I guess so, rehearsal isn't until later. What do you want to ask me?"

I went straight in. "We've heard from a few people that nobody at the theater really liked Caroline, would you say that was true?" I tried to gauge her reaction.

Gwen opened her mouth and then shut it again. "I mean, she wasn't everyone's *favorite* person, I suppose. I don't think anyone had anything against her *personally*, but she did make decisions for the theater that... unsettled people."

"Unsettled them?" Dean asked.

She shrugged. "She held the purse strings, and whenever Robert went over budget she'd come down and make cuts. She always made the hard decisions. I respected her for that, even though it pissed some people off."

"Why didn't it piss *you* off?" I asked. It seemed like out of everyone she had the most responsibility to make Robert's dreams come true. I would have thought budget cuts would anger her just as much, or even more, than the other staff.

"I worked my way up from the bottom in the theater world," she explained. "It's a privilege to be a stage manager at such an old, respected theater like this one. You know, before Robert bought the place and renamed it, the theater was called The Orville Theater. It's been here since 1931. Robert has really big dreams for this place, but theater is expensive. Sometimes wild ideas have to be reigned in back to reality."

"So you didn't have anything against Caroline at all?" Dean prodded.

Gwen frowned and shook her head. "Not really. She knew she could come to me and help talk Robert off the ledge whenever he wanted to spend crazy amounts of money on an idea. I come from the duct tape and make-it-work kinda theater environment. You know, producing grand visions with very little. She appreciated me for that."

"*Huh.*" I nodded. "But there *were* people who butted heads with Caroline, right?"

She nodded and rolled her eyes. "Oh yeah. Most of the staff, actually. Robert really propped them up and gave them high expectations of what working here would look like, and those dreams have more or less crashed and burned, I'd say."

"Anyone who you think would actually *harm* Caroline?" Dean asked.

She shifted her stance and knit her eyebrows together. "You think it was someone from the theater who...you know?"

"Killed her?" Dean added succinctly.

"It's a high possibility," I said, just to see how she responded. "It could be anyone at this point."

She pressed her lips together into a thin line. "I mean, there might have been a few arguments, but I don't think anyone would *really* harm her."

"Arguments with who? Harrison?" I asked. Tim had mentioned Harrison already.

She nodded. "And a couple others: Christina, the prop manager; Jake Amarov, lead actor; and Kirk, the wardrobe stylist."

"How heated were the arguments?" I asked.

She set down her clipboard. "Pretty heated, I guess. Nasty words were said. Caroline stormed off and had an even louder argument with Robert *about* the arguments. It was a mess."

"And when was this?" Dean asked, his pen poised on his new notepad.

She cocked her head to the side. "*Hmm*, a few weeks ago. All the disagreements have been over this latest production. It's costing more and more because Robert wants all these state of the art gimmicks, lighting, and pyrotechnics. We're way over budget as it is."

Interesting. Money issues was one of the number one reasons for divorce. And murder.

"So just for our records, where were you Friday night?" I asked dryly.

Gwen shifted her weight and rubbed her arm. "What, you mean like my alibi?"

Dean smiled. "Yep, that's what he means."

She frowned. "Oh, uh, I guess I don't have a great one. I was out with my sister for dinner, and then I went home around ten."

"Alone?" I clarified.

She nodded. "Yeah, alone."

I wrote that down in my notebook and slipped it back in my jacket pocket. "Okay, well, thanks for talking with us. You've been very helpful. Who do you think we should talk with next?"

She scoffed. "You mean, who do I think killed Caroline?"

I shrugged. "If you want to interpret it like that."

She was quiet for a minute, biting her lower lip.

"*Come on*," Dean said with a conspiratorial smirk. "There has to be someone you've had your eye on. Someone who comes to mind."

Gwen let out a deep breath. "I guess if I *had* to say someone, I would say you should talk to the two main leads, Camilla and Jake."

"And why do you say that?" I asked.

She shrugged. "Those two have the most to lose. Caroline fought with production primarily, but she clashed with the cast too. Jake especially. He's a big name already in the theater world, and he has his reputation to uphold. If this production flops, it paints a bad light on him."

"*Hmm.*" We couldn't talk to Camilla, at least not yet, but Jake wasn't off limits.

"Which way to the dressing rooms?" Dean asked.

Gwen pointed us in the right direction and we followed the winding hallways to the back of the theater, close to where we'd entered earlier.

"So what did you think of Gwen?" Dean asked when we were far enough away to not be overheard.

"I don't know," I said. "What's the motive? If she's telling the truth it seems like she had the best relationship with Caroline out of the whole staff."

Dean shook his head. "So she says. But she also had the most pressure placed on her to please Robert. Plus, she doesn't have a solid alibi. Those are pretty big red flags."

"I'm not saying we discount her, I'm just saying she's not at the top of the list right now." I stopped in my tracks and turned to Dean. He almost ran into me from the sudden pause. "I know you're trying to be helpful, Dean, but we don't have enough information yet to come to any conclusions. Throwing out wild theories doesn't help at this stage in an investigation. It just confuses things."

He frowned. "I thought this is what detecting was?"

"Right now we're just gathering facts, looking for inconsistencies. Theories come later."

He rolled his eyes. "Whatever you say, boss."

I held out for a second and then smiled. "I like when you call me boss."

He couldn't hold his composure. He smirked and said, "Noted, boss."

"Okay, back to work." I turned around and searched the many doors for Jake's name. We found the right room near the end of the hall, with his name embossed in gold letters. Fancy.

"How do we know he's here?" Dean asked.

I shrugged. "Only one way to find out." I knocked on the door and waited for a beat with no response. I knocked again and tried the knob. It opened. "Hello?" I pushed the door inward and was met with a tall, well-muscled guy wrapping a dressing robe around his frame. He had an Eastern European look to him with deathly pale skin and dark brown hair that hung over his forehead.

"Can I help you?" he asked, his voice terse.

"Sorry to intrude," Dean said with a dazzling grin. "Are you Jake?"

"What does it say on the door?" he deadpanned.

Dean faltered, not used to his charms being rejected. "Uh."

"I'm Detective Sun, and this is my partner Mr. Prescott. We'd like to talk to you for a minute about the death of Caroline Foil."

There was a shuffling sound at the back of the room behind a tall, standing partition.

Jake rolled his eyes. "You might as well come out, Richard, you're not very good at hiding."

A tall Black man who was rushing to finish buttoning his shirt moved out from behind the partition. His cheeks were flushed a deep maroon and his eyes darted from Jake to us.

"And you are?" I asked.

"Just leaving," Jake answered for him. "Bye, Richard."

The man slipped past us and practically ran out the door.

I turned to Dean, who couldn't help himself from grinning and waggling an eyebrow at me.

"Sorry to interrupt your...whatever that was," I said.

Jake let out a sigh and waved his hand in our direction. "Whatever, so what did you two want to ask me?"

"Caroline Foil. She died," Dean said.

Jake didn't seem very broken up by the news. "Yes, I know."

"How would you describe your relationship with Caroline?" I asked.

He raised an eyebrow. "My relationship? I wouldn't describe us as having *any* kind of relationship."

"But you fought with her at times," Dean pointed out, "so you clearly had some opinion of her."

"*Oh.*" He pressed his lips together. "Is that what you're here about? My little argument with her?"

I shrugged. "I wouldn't call it little. We heard it was *quite* the yelling match."

He rolled his eyes. "That woman doesn't understand art. She only sees dollar signs. I tried to explain something to her and she completely blew up for no reason. Blah, blah, blah. Budget this, budget that."

Dean looked like he wanted to say something, only he kept his mouth shut in a rare display of composure.

"So you mostly fought about money?" I clarified.

He let out a deep breath and waved his hand. "She wanted to slash the production in half. *Half.* It was ridiculous. I can't be expected to perform at my best with cheap costumes and even cheaper set design.

This isn't some community college group. People pay big money to come see a show at The Hydecker Theater."

"I'm sensing a lot of resentment," Dean said, gesturing his hand in Jake's direction. "Would you say you resented Caroline?"

Jake was clearly over talking with us. He let out a huffy breath. "Sure, whatever you want to call it."

"Just to be clear," I started. "Where were you Friday night?"

He placed his hand on his chest in mock outrage. "Are you trying to say you think I killed her? Is that what you're trying to say?"

"Um, yeah, that was kinda the idea," Dean so helpfully added.

God, why did actors have to be so dramatic?

"I was with some of my castmates at a bar downtown, if you must know. They can verify that for you," he huffed. "I might've hated that harpy, but I didn't kill Caroline. Why would I risk ruining my life on *her*?" he said the final word dripping with disdain.

"Do you know anyone who would?" I asked.

He took in a breath and let it out, calming himself. "I don't know, maybe Harrison? It's hard to imagine anyone could've killed her, but those two certainly had the most heated arguments, if that means anything to you people."

"It does," I said. "Well, thank you for your time, mister?"

He rolled his eyes again, as if we should already know. "*Amarov*. It's on the damn sign out front? Some detectives you two are."

I plastered on a fake smile and said, "Yes, of course, Mr. Amarov. If we have any more questions we'll contact you."

"Yeah, I'm sure you will." He smiled with tight eyes. "Good luck on your investigation, boys."

As we left the dressing room and slipped into the hall, Dean gave me a knowing look.

"What?" I asked.

"That man was an asshat."

I nodded in agreement. "Yep."

"*Hmm*. Do you think he was being so confrontational because he was hiding something, or was he really just that prickish?" Dean asked.

"I'd say the latter, but sometimes you get suspects who are defensive for no reason. Some people just get really scared around authority figures, or people they see as a threat."

"That makes sense." He stopped suddenly in his tracks, his eyes wide.

"What?" Was he okay? I had a short moment of panic where my heart dropped into my stomach.

"I seem to have forgotten my phone in Robert's office." He put his hands on his hips.

"*Okay?*" Was that it? Why was he being dramatic about it?

He knit his brows together. "Gosh, I really hope my phone didn't accidentally record part of Robert's conversation with Tim. That would be super embarrassing and invasive."

I frowned and crossed my arms, trying to look admonishing. "You didn't," I said.

His face broke out into a wide grin. "Oh, but I did."

"God dammit, Dean."

I knew something was up. He'd been *way* too quiet this morning. Now I knew why.

EIGHT

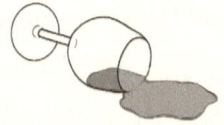

We climbed the stairs back to the second story office where Dean grabbed his phone from beneath the chair. "I am so sorry," he said. "I'm such a forgetful klutz."

Robert gave him a strange look, but didn't seem to think anything of it and went back to whatever paperwork he was so focused on.

The whole thing was ridiculous, and I should have been mad—this wasn't something I wanted Dean to make a habit of, after all—however a small part of me was intrigued. Tim had seemed very even-keeled when we'd talked to him before, but what about when it was just him and Robert? How did their dynamic change?

We walked far enough down the catwalk that we were alone, and Dean pulled out his phone with a gleeful smile.

I glared at him. "Okay, no need to gloat so hard, there's no guarantee that you even caught anything on there."

That didn't seem to deter him. He unlocked his phone and played the recording from the beginning. There was a shuffling noise as Dean oh-so-carefully dropped his phone and then lots of silence. That must have been when we were talking with Tim. Nothing interesting there. "I don't think—"

Dean shushed me, and I gave him the death stare. "Don't shush—"

He shushed me again. "Listen." In the recording Robert's office door opened and closed. Tim had walked in after we'd left.

"Mr. Hydecker, I need to talk to you," Tim's voice said, clear and bold.

"About what?" Robert replied.

"You know exactly what I want to talk about."

Robert sighed. "Can't you see that I'm already having a hard enough day as it is, Tim? Do you really need to bring this up *right now*? I thought I'd made myself clear on Wednesday."

"Well, I wasn't done talking."

Dean nudged my shoulder. "Seems like timid Tim isn't so timid after all."

I shushed him. "*Listen*," I said, mocking him.

The recording continued. "I can't give you an advance, Tim," Robert said. "Asking me again isn't going to change that fact. I'm so

100

underwater with the cost of the production, I can't afford *anything* right now."

Tim huffed. "If you could just see it from my perspective."

"My wife just died, Tim!" Robert said with a hard edge to his voice. "Can't you give me a break? I have a lot on my mind. And now Caroline might've been murdered? It's too much. You're asking too much, Tim."

"But if you just—"

"If you say one more word, Tim, I'm going to have to fire you," Robert threatened. "And that certainly wouldn't help your money troubles, would it?"

Tim grumbled, "Fine, I'll leave you alone."

In the recording the door slammed, and then it was silent again. Dean skimmed through the rest of the recording, but there was nothing else of interest. Robert had been alone in his office the rest of the time.

"Well that was something," Dean said.

"*Hmm*, that *was* something. Apparently our timid secretary has a money problem. That might be worth considering down the line." I wrote **Tim plus money** down in my notepad. It made for a good motive even if Tim did have an alibi.

"See? Aren't you glad that I did that?" Dean said with a boyish grin.

"*So glad*," I deadpanned. "Let's go find someone else to talk to."

He crossed his arms. "Who's left? Harrison?"

I shook my head. "Nah, I still want to save him for last. See what everyone else has to say about him first."

"Right, I see."

"Do you?" I asked, just to be snarky.

"Let's go, then." Dean pushed my shoulder and walked ahead of me toward the winding stairs.

We wandered around the back halls reading off the signs on each door until we found one for the costume department. We walked inside and looked around, but it was empty. "It looks like no one's home," Dean said.

"So let's go find them." There was nobody in the hallway, and there was nobody in any of the open rooms.

"Outside?" Dean suggested.

He pushed open the metal door that led to the back parking lot. A wave of cigarette smoke hit me. There was a man and a woman smoking up against the back of the building. These two just might be who we were looking for. "Hey there," Dean said.

The man looked over, his eyes trailing up and down. "Can we help you?"

"Hopefully," I said. "Do you two work here?"

The man hesitated before saying, "Yeah. Who are you?"

"I'm Detective Sun and this is my assistant detective Mr. Prescott. We've been hired by Mr. Hydecker to look into the circumstances surrounding his wife's death."

The man nodded, but he didn't look any more at ease. "Okay. I'm Kirk Landry, the costume designer." Kirk was a tall, lanky Black man in his forties. He was dressed in crimson trousers and a matching silk dress shirt, coordinated with a gold watch and gold hoop earrings. Based on the spit shine of his shoes and the timepiece on his wrist, he had money. So why was he smoking at the back of a broke theater?

I looked to the woman for a reply, who hadn't said anything at all yet. "I'm Christina Fogel, prop manager." She was stocky and short with messy blonde hair up in a ponytail. She was wearing tan overalls and heavy workman's boots.

"Nice to meet you both," I said, "We just want to ask you guys a few questions, if you don't mind?"

"Sure," Kirk said, less than thrilled.

Dean started us off, "Would you say that you knew Caroline well?"

Kirk shook his head. "Not really."

Not much of a talker was he? At least he was answering, unlike Christina.

"Did you witness any of the arguments between Caroline and the other members of the staff?" I asked. "Or did you ever argue with her yourself?"

"Define *argue*," Christina said before taking another drag from her lit cigarette.

"Okay." I crossed my arms. "I would define an argument as a discussion that got heated. Did you ever have one of those?"

Neither of them said anything right away, which meant the answer was probably yes.

"I might've talked to her a few times in a way that some could interpret as an argument," Kirk replied, looking down at the ground.

"About what?" Dean asked. "The budget?"

"I see you've been talking to the rest of the staff," he said. "Yes, our discussions were always about money. Caroline was constantly trying to cut the budget to the wardrobe department. And every department, really. At times it made me very upset. I was told when Robert hired me that I would have a large fund for the costumes set aside to make his production everything that it needed to be. Then, as soon as I got here I found out that was not the case. His wife had our production on a leash, and she was not afraid to choke us if she needed to."

The woman the staff of the theater was describing didn't resonate at all with the woman I'd met at the club just two days ago. Who was the *real* Caroline?

I turned to Christina. "Did you have similar arguments with Caroline?"

She shrugged. "I guess you could say that."

"Also about money?" I confirmed.

Color flushed her cheeks. "It wasn't just about the money," she said curtly. "Robert wanted certain stunts to be performed in the show, and Caroline wanted to slash the budget on those as well. Which wasn't just *annoying*, it was very dangerous. We were supposed to have multiple trap doors in the floor for a quick drop stunt, and she didn't want to pay the money that it was going to take to make sure that those stunts were done safely."

Dean smiled. "Yes, we've gathered that not very many people here were happy with her changes. Can you think of anyone who might have been upset enough to do something about it?"

"You mean like harm her?" Kirk asked.

Dean nodded.

The pair looked at each other and thought for a moment. It looked like Kirk wanted to say something, but held back.

"What?" I asked.

He shrugged. "I don't know. I just can't believe that anyone would actually harm her, but there was something said during an argument that could be *interpreted* as a threat."

"Was this from Harrison?" I asked. "We've heard a couple things about him today."

Christina and Kirk both nodded.

"What was the threat?" Dean asked.

Kirk rolled his eyes. "I mean, it was silly. It's not as if he actually meant it. In the heat of the moment he said something like, *if you change one more goddamn thing about the show I'm gonna kill you.* You know, something like that."

"Sure."

Kirk stubbed out his cigarette and crossed his arms. "Was that all that you wanted to know?"

"Not quite, "I said. "Where were you Friday night around eleven o'clock?"

His eyes widened. "You mean when Caroline was killed?"

Dean smiled. "Why does everyone keep acting so surprised when we want to know their alibi? This is a murder investigation."

Normally I'd give him a dark look for him to shut up, but in this case I was interested in what the pair had to say in reply.

Kirk cleared his throat. "I was at home all evening with my husband. He can verify that I never left the house."

"Okay." I wrote down his alibi and looked to Christina. "And you?" I asked.

She placed a hand on her hip and shifted her stance. "I was at a cabin upstate with my boyfriend over the weekend. So I wasn't even in town when Caroline was killed."

How convenient. "Okay, we'll check on those alibis. Thanks for taking the time to speak with us. We'll let you know if we have any more questions down the line."

Neither seemed thrilled that I'd be verifying their stories.

"Is Harrison here today?" Dean asked, breaking the tension.

They both nodded and Kirk said, "Yep, he's up in the lighting booth. He practically lives up there."

"Thanks, we'll speak to him next." I gave them a curt smile and followed Dean back into the building.

When we were far enough away Dean asked, "So what did we think of them?"

I shook my head. I don't know. It seems kind of strange that everyone with motive somehow has an ironclad alibi. I can sense we're going to be doing a lot of double-checking on this case."

"Great," Dean said. "I've been practicing my voices in case I need to call people."

"Your voices?" I asked, totally confused as to what he was talking about.

He screwed up his nose and lowered the pitch of his voice, "This is Detective Warner calling from the Hollywood Police Department, can you confirm something for me?"

It was a terrible likeness, which made me laugh.

Dean grinned. "What? You don't think it would work?"

"It might work, but you don't sound anything like Warner," I said. "And I mean that as a compliment."

He shrugged, conflicted. "Thanks?"

"You're welcome, now let's go find this guy. He might be exactly what we're looking for."

We passed through a doorway into the auditorium section of the theater. There must have been over a thousand seats. The space was grand with gold molding on the walls and plush red velvet carpets and upholstery.

Up on stage, there were several pieces of Victorian furniture arranged in a square, along with a few old Turkish rugs on the floor. Standing walls covered in ornate wallpaper framed the fake living room. Gwen had made it seem like they would be doing rehearsals later, even with everything going on.

Dean shoved through a door marked *employees only* to a dark staircase that led up to the second floor balcony. There were one or two small empty offices, a supply closet, and one main door in the middle of the hallway. "I assume that's the control booth?" I asked.

Dean shrugged. "Your guess is as good as mine," he said. "I like watching plays, I've never put one on before."

"Really?" I said. "You kinda strike me as a theater kid."

He raised one brow. "I don't know if I should take that as a compliment or a dig."

I shook my head. "Take it however you want to take it."

He grinned. "Fine, compliment, then."

We knocked on the door and waited for a reply. When no one answered, Dean pushed inside. The room was pitch black. I felt around for a light switch and flicked it on.

"Hey, what the hell?" a deep, gravelly voice said.

There was a man lying down in a collapsible cot in the corner; dark sheets covered his tall frame.

"Sorry," Dean said. "We didn't realize someone was sleeping here. Are you Harrison?"

"Who's asking?" He looked between us warily. He had pale, almost paper white skin, shoulder-length dark hair, a five-o'clock shadow, and was wearing a rumpled black T-shirt with gray pants.

The room was small and cramped with equipment—control panels, dimmers, and complex switches for the lights. A laptop and a mostly empty mug of coffee sat on the table amongst the chaos.

I explained our credentials once again.

He pulled the sheets aside and stood up. "Detectives, huh? I didn't think Robert would shell out the money for that sort of thing."

"Even to investigate his own wife's murder?" Dean asked.

Harrison shrugged. "Everyone knew he was dating Camilla. I would think he would be glad that Caroline is gone."

"Are *you*?" I asked.

Again, he shrugged. "I'm not *not* happy, if that's what you're asking."

"No love lost, it sounds like?" Dean asked.

He scoffed. "Hell no. I hated Caroline, as I'm sure everyone has already told you, which is why you're here in the first place."

Well I guess we didn't need to beat around the bush. He was clearly open to talking about it. "What did you two argue about the most?" I asked.

He frowned. "What else? *Money*. Caroline wanted to keep the visual effects to a minimum, which would have changed the entire show. Robert wanted to use a set piece where different colored lights followed different characters around the stage to signify their struggles through the patriarchy. It was all very new and exciting. Caroline didn't want to spend to upgrade the lights to the new standard, so I'm stuck with these old dinosaurs that keep breaking down," he pointed to a lone caster light sitting on the floor, "that haven't been replaced since the eighties. It was gonna cause a fire one of these days if we didn't address the issue. She wasn't having it."

Hmm. Every single person who worked at the theater had said the same thing about Caroline Foil. She wasn't concerned about the theater or the show, she was only worried about the cost of everything. It made me wonder if she'd had more money issues than either Dean or I realized.

"Is that when you said that you wanted to kill her?" Dean asked.

Harrison rolled his eyes. "That's so idiotic. Yes, I said that, but you can't *seriously* believe that just because I said I wanted to kill her I would *actually* kill her."

Dean shrugged. "You'd be surprised how many times a threat is acted on."

"This isn't a movie," Harrison argued. "And I didn't kill her. I didn't even know she was dead until this morning when Gwen told me."

"So where were you Friday night?" I asked.

He crossed his arms and stared me down, obviously not intimidated by us in the slightest. "I was with a friend, if you must know."

Dean nodded. "We must."

"All night?" I confirmed.

He gave a vague, noncommittal shrug. "Most of the night."

"So what does *most of the night* mean to you? What about around ten o'clock?"

"I don't know." He shook his head. "I was kind of out of it. You'll have to ask my friend."

"Can we get their contact information?" Dean asked.

Harrison searched around for a pen and paper with no luck. I didn't know how you'd find *anything* in the cramped space. Eventually, I felt bad for him, and I held out my notepad for him to write down the name and number.

"So if not you, then who do you think hated Caroline enough to harm her?" I asked. It was the same question we'd asked everyone else today, except everyone else had said Harrison's name, so his answer would be even more intriguing.

He rubbed his hands together. "I don't know, man. I think it could be that assistant."

"The assistant?" Dean asked. "Do you mean Heather?"

He nodded. "Yeah, the pretty one."

"Why do you think it could be her?" I asked. His answer had come so far out of left field.

"I saw her one day with a bunch of notes. You know, blackmail notes."

"You knew about the letters?" Dean asked with a raised eyebrow.

He nodded. "I knew *someone* was blackmailing her. And no, I had no idea what it was about, if that's your next question."

It *was* my next question. "Why do you think Heather sent them?"

"Because think about it: Heather was around Caroline twenty-four seven. She probably knew more about Caroline than her own husband. If anyone had dirt on Caroline, it was her."

"So you think Heather was the blackmailer," I said. "Do you think she could have killed her too?"

He gestured with his hand. "Naturally."

"But why?" Dean asked. Clearly he wasn't buying into Harrison's theory.

"Why else?" he replied. "Caroline must have stopped paying, right? The cost of the production was getting so high she must've gotten fed up and started ignoring the blackmailer. Heather had to have realized she couldn't get any more out of Caroline, so she killed her."

"Why would that solve her problem? I asked, unable to follow his logic. "Wouldn't that just take away her extra income?"

He raised a finger and gave us a crooked smile. "Ah, but do you know about the will?"

Dean and I shared a look. "What will?" I asked.

Harrison grinned with satisfaction. "There was a rumor going around the theater that because Robert was cheating on his wife, Caroline wrote a new will that cut him out completely. I wouldn't be surprised if Heather was mentioned as an inheritor on that new document."

This was surprising news. No one had mentioned a will, not even Heather. I still thought Heather as the killer was a bad theory, but the will added a whole new dimension to the case.

"Thanks for that information," I said. "We'll be checking into your alibi. I hope I don't have to say it, but, don't leave town, okay?"

Harrison rolled his eyes and scoffed. "Okay, man, whatever you say. But I'm telling you, everyone else is throwing me under the bus because they're keeping secrets from you."

"What kind of secrets?" Dean asked.

Harrison jutted his chin out. "I don't know, you're the detectives."

Very helpful.

"We'll contact you if we have any more questions," I said. "We'll let you get back to your nap."

When we left the control booth Dean had a stupid grin on his face.

"What?" I asked.

"The will!"

"Yeah, I know. I didn't see that coming. And why did Heather hide it from us? Unless she didn't know about it, which I would find highly unlikely."

"*Hmm*, I know. It couldn't be Heather, though, right?" Dean pondered aloud. "Why the hell would she reach out and hire us if she was the blackmailer, or even the killer? It just doesn't make sense."

"I don't know." I shrugged. "I mean, she's smart enough to make a power move like that, but I just don't see it. Let's keep this new information to ourselves for now."

Dean snapped his fingers. "So we can use it later."

I nodded, holding back a smile. "Yeah, that's the general idea, Dean."

"I'm hungry," Dean announced as we made our way down the stairs back to the lobby.

"You're always hungry."

"*Feed me Seymour!*" he cried.

I couldn't help but grin full force. "See? I knew you were a theater kid!"

He frowned, and then brightened again just as fast. "But you knew the reference, didn't you?" he asked, hanging onto my shoulder.

"Let's go get some burgers and talk over what we know so far," I said, walking in the direction of the exit.

He beamed and jogged to catch up to me. "You're avoiding my comment, but I don't care because I agree."

I chuckled. "Come on, you pain in the ass."

NINE

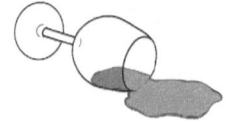

"You're a doll, Rosalie," Dean said with a smile, accepting the plate stacked high with a burger and fries.

Rosalie, as usual, wasn't moved by his charms whatsoever. She was an emotional brick of a woman who treated her customers at Greta's diner with transparent contempt. "Will that be all?" she asked in a dull, you're-wasting-my-time tone.

"We're good," I answered for him before he could continue an already dead conversation.

She plastered on a fake smile as she walked away to another table.

Dean nodded. "Charming woman."

"Don't aggravate Rosalie," I warned him. "I like this place, and I don't want to have to find a new spot."

He placed his hand on his chest in mock outrage and furrowed his brow. "What did I do?"

"Hey, guys," Lexi said as she crammed into the booth beside me, pushing me over to the window. She was huffing and puffing like she was out of breath, and when I looked down I saw why. Captain, my black labradoodle, was beneath the table wagging his tail from what was, no doubt, an energetic walk.

"Thanks for meeting us," I said, leaning across her to scratch Captain's face.

"No problem. You're saving me, really," she said.

Technically, according to her father—my brother Mark—she wasn't supposed to be working at the office for a while so she could study and focus on her college application prep. But how was I going to tell her no? She was a damn good researcher and an important part of the team.

"What did you guys learn today?" she asked.

Dean grinned conspiratorially. "You won't believe what we just heard." He paused for dramatic effect.

She waved her hand. "Yes?"

"Caroline had a secret will," I said, stealing the wind from his sails.

Dean gave me the death glare. "That was *my* line."

I shrugged and took a bite from my sandwich—ham and tomato on rye, lots of mayo, hold the onion.

Lexi gasped. "*No.*"

Dean nodded maniacally. "Yes."

"That changes everything."

I hummed in agreement. "If Caroline had a secret will and was going to write Robert out to add someone new, the killer *must* have known about it," I argued. "Otherwise it would have been a dumb move on their part to get rid of her. Unless, the killer was Robert, and we already know that couldn't be true because he has an airtight alibi."

"What's a better alibi than having a private detective watching you while your wife is being murdered?" Dean said.

Lexi shrugged. "It's almost *too* good."

Dean nodded and shoved a handful of fries into his mouth. "I know, I was thinking about that this morning, but *grumpy* over here doesn't think it's possible."

I frowned at him.

"And after today," he continued, "I'm starting to agree with him. This new will is a game changer. We need to find it."

Lexi turned to me. "Do you know her lawyers? Aren't they obligated to tell you who was added?"

I cocked my head to the side. "Not always. It's a tricky legal loophole. Warner might be able to force them to tell him if he gets a court order. But me? I don't think so."

Lexi pulled out her phone. "What's the name? Let me try something."

I was skeptical, but I'd seen her do more with less, so I gave her the name and watched her work.

She called the number and smiled wide, getting into character. "Hello, Dellany and Goldberg? Uh-huh, this is Sarah Witten with Schuster and Meyers. I'm calling to inquire about Caroline Foil's estate." There was a long pause. Maybe she was being transferred? She introduced herself again and asked about Caroline's inheritors. Then she named off a jumble of legal terms that surprised me. What was this kid doing with her free time? "Of course I understand you can't disclose that information without cause. Can you tell me what date the new policy went into effect? *Mmm-hmm*. Yes, thank you so much. Mr. Meyers appreciates it."

She hung up the phone and shrugged. "They wouldn't tell me anything about what was actually *in* the policy, but they told me when it was changed—two weeks ago."

"Two weeks, huh?" Dean said. "That's not very long ago. What if our killer *didn't* know about the change?"

"Or what if they were waiting for it before making their move," I replied. "That's more likely."

"But it had to be someone close to Caroline, right?" Lexi said. "Otherwise how would they know about her plan?"

I took another bite of my sandwich. "Well, everyone at the theater apparently knew, so it wasn't much of a secret. I don't know *how* they knew, but they knew."

"Robert didn't know, right?" she said.

I raised a hand. "He didn't *mention* it, that doesn't mean that he didn't know about it. Maybe he was embarrassed."

"True," she conceded.

"So what you're saying is...this information doesn't help us narrow down our suspect pool whatsoever?" Dean said with pinched brows.

I shrugged. "*Eh*, I mean, it certainly adds motive. Plus, the killer couldn't have been *anyone*. It had to have been someone close enough to Caroline for her to add them to her will."

"So not Harrison, not Christina," Dean said, dipping his fries in ketchup. "None of the people she fought with?"

"They would be *highly* unlikely candidates," I said.

Dean let out a sigh. "Also, if it *was* the blackmailer who killed her like Harrison suggested, then why? That's a pretty dumb thing to do."

I leaned back in the seat. "I don't know, maybe they sensed that she wasn't going to keep paying, and so they manipulated her into adding them to her will for one big payday?"

"If you assume the blackmailer is someone close to her," Lexi added.

"Well they must be, right?" I said. "Heather said she didn't know what Caroline was actually being blackmailed over, but it had to be something convincing enough for her to pay out for months on end. There was a whole stack of notes."

Dean shook his head. "It would be interesting if it was Heather, but I still think she's too sweet. Unless she's hiding a big secret from us."

"Who else was close to Caroline?" Lexi asked, snagging a fry from Dean's plate.

I crossed my arms. "Well no one at the theater liked her, it seems like Robert didn't like her, and she didn't have many friends. Who's left?"

"Maybe *I* did it," Dean said.

Lexi laughed. "Shut up you dork. This is serious."

Dean simmered down, but he was still smiling under the surface. "I really don't know who else was in her life that we haven't already talked to."

"We still haven't talked to Camilla," I brought up. "I know Robert said he didn't want us to, but he couldn't really be serious? This is a murder investigation. Of course we're going to talk to her, even if she does have an airtight alibi."

Dean leaned down and fed Captain a french fry under the table.

I frowned. "Don't make my dog fat, Dean."

He pinched his brows and laughed. "I would never make him fat." He smooshed Captain's smiling face. "Would I? You stinkin' cutie."

I rolled my eyes and tried not to smile, failing miserably. I'd had my doubts about hiring Dean, but seeing how he interacted with Lexi and

Captain made my heart sing. I was quickly becoming attached to him. And that scared me.

I cleared my throat and pushed away my mostly uneaten sandwich. "We better get a move on. We need to talk to Camilla and then decide our next move."

Lexi looked up from her phone and waved it. "I already found her address. She's in Hollywood, so not too far from the theater."

"How could you possibly have already found her address?" Dean asked. "We're still eating lunch."

"*You* are still eating lunch," I pointed out. I was done.

"Whatever."

Lexi smiled at us and leaned down to ruffle Captain's fur. "I'll take Captain back to your apartment, and then I have Korean lessons."

"Korean lessons?" I asked. That was the first I was hearing about any lessons.

She rolled her eyes. "Yeah, Dad is making me take lessons with a Korean tutor. He wants me to be able to talk to Grandpa in Korean for his birthday.

"Interesting." My dad hadn't been all that concerned with Mark and I learning Korean when we were kids, so I didn't see why Mark was insisting Lexi tack that onto her already busy schedule. Not that learning Korean was a bad thing. I kinda wished that I'd learned more when I was a kid. I often felt a disconnect from others in my community, but then again, any actual Korean just saw me as some half-white American no matter what I did, so learning more Korean wouldn't really help me much.

Lexi grinned and stole a couple more fries from Dean's plate for the road. "Wish me luck."

I nodded. "Good luck, not that you need it."

"I texted you that address," she said before she slipped away with Captain nipping at her heels.

"Bye, buddy," Dean called as they left.

"You know, Lexi's right," I said. "You *are* a dork."

He grinned even harder. "Thanks."

* * *

Camilla Martínez Lived in West Hollywood, not far from the gay epicenter of LA. The duplex was small, but nice. I could imagine from the location and style that it must have been expensive, although not outlandish. It was still a duplex in the city, not a mansion up in the hills, hidden behind closed gates.

Dean knocked on the door and we waited. It didn't take her long to answer, with wet hair and a bathrobe tied around her middle. "Camilla Martínez?" he asked.

She immediately frowned. "Who's asking?"

I jumped in. "I'm Detective Sun from The Golden Sun Detective Agency. Robert Hydecker hired us to look into the death of his wife. Do you have a few minutes to talk to us?"

She stared at me for a painful second. "Oh...sure. Come on in, I guess."

We entered the living room. It was all white and gold, very well decorated—expensive. You wouldn't know from the outside. She directed us to a plush white sofa and we sat down across from her.

She pulled her hair over her shoulder. "So what do you want to ask me?"

"You were dating Robert, correct?" I asked, just to get the ball rolling. Obviously we knew she was dating Robert, but it was good to get her sense of things, her perspective.

She shrugged. "I guess you could call it that."

"You wouldn't?" Dean asked.

"*Hmm*, we were seeing each other regularly, does that count as dating?" she asked, playing with a knot in her long, dark locks.

"To some people," I said. "And how long have you been *seeing* him?"

She looked up in thought. "Maybe two months? Around the time I auditioned for the show. Which was one of the reasons Robert wanted to keep us a secret. Obviously he didn't want his wife to know, but on top of that, if the news spread people would question why I got the lead part. It had *nothing* to do with my relationship with Robert," she said firmly.

Was she trying to convince *us*, or herself?

"I see, and did you get the impression that Caroline knew about the affair?" I asked.

She nodded. "Robert was hell-bent on believing that she didn't, but I knew she did. A woman always knows. The way she looked at me whenever she visited the theater, whenever she visited Robert. They also fought a lot."

Dean raised a brow. "About you?"

She shook her head. "No, mostly about the theater. I'm just saying that they fought a lot in general."

"We also got the impression that everyone else at the theater knew about the affair as well ," I said. "Would you say that's true?"

"I guess so," she said. "Robert wasn't really that great at hiding it, to be honest. He thought he was, but he wasn't. He planned lots of little trips and talked about them as if people didn't realize they were for the both of us. It didn't take a genius to figure it out."

"*Uh-huh*, and how was your relationship with Caroline?" I asked. "We've heard that she had a lot of arguments with the staff of the theater. How about you?"

She let out a deep breath. "She never fought with me. Maybe she saw it as a losing battle, but she never took out her frustrations on me. I don't know why. Maybe she would've had to acknowledge the affair that way. She thought she was keeping it hidden or something if she didn't react. If anything, it actually made it more obvious because I was the only one in the theater she *didn't* argue with. It singled me out."

"So you're saying you didn't have anything against Caroline?" Dean asked.

She rolled her shoulder. "Why would I?"

I almost laughed. "I mean, she *was* the wife of the guy you were dating. You didn't harbor any resentment against her? Wish that they would get divorced?"

She frowned and pinched her brows. "No, never. Are you trying to ask if I killed her?"

Dean shrugged ever so helpfully.

"Well I didn't," she said. "I like going on dates with Robert because of what he brings to the table, and behind every wealthy man is a smart woman. Robert might have been *spending* the money, but Caroline was *making* the money. Why would I want to sever that relationship?"

That painted a very clear picture of her intentions and motivations. It was curious that she didn't even try and lie about it, most people would. "So you're saying it would've been dumb on your part to kill her?"

She rolled her wrist. "Exactly. How would killing Caroline benefit me?"

"So if not you, then who do you think wanted to harm her?" I asked —the same question I'd asked everyone.

She thought for a second and cocked her head to the side. "I think it was a woman," she replied.

"Really?" Dean asked. "How come?"

"Well, she was poisoned, right?" She raised a brow. "Overdosed and then pushed into the pool? That's a very passive, female way to kill someone. A man would have just shot her and been done with it."

That was certainly food for thought. "So you think we're either looking for a woman or a very passive man?" I asked.

"Maybe it was Tim," she said. "If you're looking for a passive man, Tim is as passive as it gets."

Clearly Camilla didn't know about Tim's other side, the side we'd heard in Dean's recording. Tim wasn't afraid to get loud when he was backed into a corner, when he was scared.

"Interesting, so what woman do you think would have killed Caroline?" I asked as a follow-up question.

She hummed and then said, "Heather probably. She was the closest person to Caroline and could have gotten into the house while Robert and I were in Newport."

"But what's the motive?" Dean asked.

Camilla scoffed. "After spending twelve hours a day with that woman, I would want some revenge too. She probably killed her just so she could get some damn vacation time."

Not a strong motive, and yet anything is possible in the right circumstances. Could Heather have snapped? She didn't seem like the type, although I'd been wrong before. That was the second time that someone had suggested Heather could have been a killer. Was there merit to that? Or was it a coincidence? It seemed like Heather was the closest thing Caroline had to a friend, so maybe it wasn't so crazy an idea.

"Well, thanks for answering our questions," I said. "You've been very helpful."

"Don't you want to know about my alibi?" she asked, her brow furrowed.

So Robert hadn't told her about Caroline hiring us to follow them. "You said you and Robert were in Newport?" I asked.

She nodded. "Yes, all night."

I crossed my arms. "Neither of you left the hotel, even for a moment?"

"We went dancing at a club, had dinner at the hotel, and didn't leave until the morning," she said. "I'm sure there's easy ways of confirming that."

"*Very* easy ways," Dean said with a smirk.

I gave him a quick shake of my head and stood up from the couch. "That's all, Ms. Martínez. If we have any more questions we'll contact you."

We left the house and got back in the Jeep. Dean ran a hand through his chestnut waves. "Well that was interesting. Two people think Heather could have killed Caroline? Are we buying that?"

I shook my head. "I don't know. It does check a couple boxes. I mean, she *was* the closest person to Caroline which means she knew about the blackmail, and she probably knew about the will and just decided not to tell us. Let's test our theory, shall we?" I pulled out my phone and typed a quick text message to Heather.

N: Is there anything that you want to tell us? Something you maybe withheld?

It didn't take long for her to reply.

H: Can you meet me at the club? First thing tomorrow morning?

I frowned. "Well, she took the bait." I showed Dean her reply.

Dean pressed his lips together. "That's not good, is it?"

I shrugged. "I kept it vague on purpose. It's possible that she's referencing something completely different."

He pulled his brows together. "Is it though?"

"I guess we'll find out. The club." I frowned. "Does this mean that I have to put on a stupid suit again?"

Dean grinned a toothy smile. "Ah, I know just the one."

"God, I think a small part of you enjoys torturing me."

"A *small* part?" he said with a laugh.

"Whatever." I rolled my eyes, started the car, and drove it back towards the office, the LA sunset cutting across the hills.

Whatever she was going to tell us, I had a bad feeling about it.

TEN

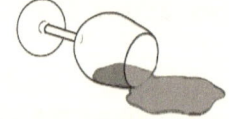

The following morning, Dean dressed me in the silliest suit he could find, which happened to be a pale pink with darker pink piping. It was like a costume from a movie, not something your average guy wore to the club. Dean shrugged when he caught my expression of obvious discontent. "What? It's my roomiest suit, you complained that the other one was too tight in the shoulders."

"So this is the compromise?"

He grinned. "Hey, I offered to give you the name of my tailor."

I frowned. "Do I look like I have the money for a bespoke suit right now?"

"*Oh,*" he smiled widely, "he knows the word *bespoke*. Maybe you're not a total lost cause."

I sighed. "Can we get on with this?"

"Please, by all means. Pick a tie." Dean pulled out a retractable hanging rack from his large walk-in closet that was filled with ties. There had to be about a hundred.

"Spent your blood money wisely, did you?" I said gruffly.

"Ha, ha. Just because you don't appreciate the finer things in life, doesn't mean my lifestyle is so silly," Dean quipped. "We're in Hollywood, after all."

"Whatever." I chose a tie at random, only Dean plucked it from my hand, quickly replacing it with another.

"This one's better."

I frowned. "I don't like when other people make decisions for me, Dean," I said, grabbing the original tie again.

He threw up his hands in defense. "Fine, have it your way."

"*Thanks*, I will." I tied the navy blue tie around my throat as we walked out of the room.

The front door to the apartment opened, and Fern walked in, a vision in turquoise.

She breathed out a long, relaxed breath and threw her wide-brimmed hat on the sofa. "Hello boys, have you solved it yet?"

Dean smiled. "Not quite, darling, but we're almost there. How was the shoot?"

Fern's switch from conning to fashion was an interesting transition.

She flashed a brilliant smile of white teeth and waved her hand through the air. "Amazing. The designer is an absolute dream. He really takes all my suggestions. He says I'm his ultimate muse."

"How much is being a muse paying these days?" I asked.

Fern frowned at my cynicism. "I ate at the Ritz for lunch, and Giovanni gifted me this dress. I imagine it'll fetch a pretty penny online."

"Is that taxable income?" I joked.

She rolled her eyes. "I'm just starting in a new career, I'm still finding my sea legs."

I was surprised that Fern would admit to any kind of struggle, much less to me of all people.

"You're doing amazing, darling, one step at a time," Dean said, giving me a dirty look before smiling back at Fern. "Today you're a muse, tomorrow you're a mogul."

She flicked her hand through the air. "Naturally."

"We need to go," I reminded him.

"Yes, fine." He kissed Fern on the cheek and we left for the club.

* * *

It was late in the morning now, closer to brunch than breakfast. Dean got us a seat at the bar where I ordered a Coke, and Dean ordered a vodka soda. The bar had a polished wooden bar top, lots of gold accents, and moody lighting—very high-end. The Coke was...a Coke.

"We're working," I said. "You shouldn't be drinking."

Dean shrugged. "Why not? Maybe a drink is exactly what we need to lull Heather into telling us whatever she's been keeping secret."

I shook my head. "I told you before, that doesn't work. You just get drunk suspects, not loose lips. Besides, it's not five o'clock yet."

"Whatever. It's five o'clock somewhere."

I looked down at my phone. Heather was late. It was ten minutes past noon. I also had two text notifications, both from my mom asking if I had time for lunch this week. I deleted the notifications and locked my phone.

"So, Noah," Dean started.

"Yes?" I asked, taking a long sip from my drink.

"Let's revisit this whole no-dating-in-the-office thing. What's up with that?"

I sighed. "You know what's up with that. You already asked me about this."

"I'm just trying to understand," he said innocently. "Is it that you didn't *like* the kiss?"

I flushed and cleared my throat. "What?"

"The kiss? Was it bad or something? Is that why you won't go on a real date with me?"

The pink suit was suddenly feeling quite snug around my chest. "Come on, Dean. We're supposed to be working here."

He waved his hand at the empty bar. "And yet, Heather is nowhere to be found."

It was odd, why tell us to meet her here and then ditch her own meeting? Had she gotten cold feet?

"The kiss was...fine," I said after a beat.

Dean furrowed his brow. "Wow, way to make a guy feel good about himself. *Fine? It was fine?*"

I flushed even harder. "You know, normal."

"Fine and normal are not filling me with confidence, Noah." He shook his head.

"Good, they're not supposed to, because we're *not* dating."

"So you just want to forget about it?" he asked.

I nodded and took another sip of Coke. "Yes, that was kind of the idea."

He went silent, and I was worried that maybe I'd hurt his feelings for real, but then he smiled. "Fine. I won't tell you what *I* thought of the kiss, then. I'll just move on, and we'll be two working professionals."

I cleared my throat and jerked my chin up. "Good."

He went quiet, waiting for me to take the bait.

After a beat I rolled my eyes and said, "Are *you* trying to say that you thought the kiss was bad?"

He grinned and leaned in closer, close enough to feel his breath on my neck. "No."

I ran a nervous hand across my short-cropped buzzcut. Where was Heather? "I don't think she's coming," I said to change the subject.

Dean pulled away a safe distance and nodded. "I agree. She's playing with us, which doesn't seem like a very innocent-person thing to do. I'm very confused."

We waited around for a total of half an hour before calling it. My coke was empty and the ice had melted. "Let's go pay our client a visit, shall we?" I suggested. If she was going to dangle crucial information in front of us, we were going to have to go get it ourselves.

Dean nodded in agreement. "Let's."

Dean paid his tab, and I handed him a few bucks in cash. "What's this for?" he asked—as if he didn't know.

"The Coke," I deadpanned.

"Oh." He accepted the money, only as soon as we got into the Jeep I caught him stuffing the bills into the center console.

"I saw that," I said.

He smiled innocently, batting his long lashes. "Saw what?"

I rolled my eyes. "You're such a pain in my ass."

"*Well someone's gotta do it,*" he mumbled.

"What?"

He grinned and clicked in his seatbelt. "Nothing."

***

It wasn't hard to get Heather's address. All I had to do was text Robert. Heather lived in Glendale. Not close to the magazine's office downtown, but close enough to Caroline and Robert's house in the hills. It was a small, average apartment building much like Dean's—no concierge or fancy amenities, but nice.

We took the elevator to the top floor and stood outside her apartment. Dean knocked. No answer. "Maybe she's not home?" Dean suggested.

I knocked again. "She's home."

"How do you know?"

"I saw her car in the parking lot as we pulled up," I said, remembering her bright blue Prius from when she'd paid us a visit at the office.

Dean shrugged. "Maybe she got a cab? Maybe she's out with a friend?"

I frowned. "Stop playing devil's advocate for one second. The simplest answer is usually the truth."

He furrowed his brow. "So she's not answering because?"

I grumbled something incoherent and tried the door knob. It turned easily in my hand.

Dean gasped. "Did you just break and enter, detective?"

I narrowed my eyes at him as I pushed in the door. "Hello?" I called. "Heather?"

136

Immediately I could tell the apartment had been trashed. My foot bumped into a fallen potted plant, dirt spilled all over the carpet. Furniture was knocked over, there were papers and books strewn everywhere, and even the blinds had been pulled from their place on the wall.

"What the hell?" Dean said as he followed behind me.

"This does not feel good." We walked another few feet into the apartment and found the body in the living room.

"Dammit!" Dean rushed over and knelt beside the body.

"Don't touch anything," I warned.

He whipped his head back to look at me. "I wasn't going to."

He definitely *was* going to. I pulled a set of latex gloves from my back pocket and handed him one of them, taking the other for myself. "Here. Put your other hand in your pocket or something."

He frowned. "I'm not a child."

"Could have fooled me," I said under my breath.

"How did she die?" Dean asked, surveying the body. Heather was face down on the carpet, her limbs splayed.

I pointed at an open plastic bag of a powdery white substance. "I'm guessing that's not flour."

Dean leaned down and looked at it closer. "Yeah, that's definitely cocaine, probably laced with fentanyl or something else bad. It wouldn't take much."

"Heather did not strike me as a drug addict, you?" I asked.

He shook his head. "No, not at all. This is obviously a cover-up. No way this was a genuine overdose. Why would she have trashed her own apartment?"

He was right. It didn't add up, whatsoever. "Someone must've known that she had a key piece of information she was going to share with us. And they silenced her for it."

"I think I see something." Dean reached under Heather's frame with his gloved hand and pulled out a phone. "She must've fallen on top of it during the struggle. The killer got lazy."

"Or they were worried about time." He handed the phone to me. I remembered her passcode from when she was in the office earlier. "One, one, one, one." Not a great choice. "Here's her messages to us." Dean looked over my shoulder as I scrolled through the text thread. "There's one more she didn't send."

Caroline had a boyfriend, I know who it was.

"Oh my God," Dean said beside me. "They were *both* having affairs?"

"Question is, why was this something to kill her over?" I asked aloud. "Unless this secret boyfriend is the one who killed Caroline."

Dean frowned. "How did they figure out that Heather was going to tell us today? Was it a coincidence?"

I shook my head. "You know I don't believe in those. No, someone knew. Someone close to Heather, close to everything."

"It had to be somebody from the theater, right?" Dean asked, "We stirred something up by asking all those questions."

I caught Dean's eye. "This is *not* our fault. I won't have you thinking that." He shrugged and looked away. "We didn't know Heather had more information she was keeping from us," I said. "How could we have known she was in danger? Everyone else at the theater already knew about Camilla and about all the arguments."

"Not the blackmail, though," Dean pointed out. "Only a few knew about that. Harrison being one."

"You think Harrison could have been the secret boyfriend?" I asked. "Then what was all that fighting about? A ruse?"

He shrugged. "Possibly, or maybe it was just a toxic relationship bubbling to the surface, revealing itself."

"Maybe." I looked around at the apartment once more. "What were they looking for, though? The will? Why would Heather have it? Shouldn't the lawyer be keeping it safe somewhere?"

Dean sucked on his teeth. "Well, you saw how that went earlier when Lexi tried to ask about it. The killer probably couldn't get their hands on the will just like we couldn't. They must be trying to find Caroline's personal copy."

"*Hmm*, Caroline's house wasn't trashed, though," I pointed out. Why go through the effort of killing her and then not look through the house? Had they been interrupted? Or something else?

He shrugged. "They could be searching it right now."

I pulled out my phone. "We need to call this in. Warner is going to have a field day."

"Why?" Dean asked. "*Other than the obvious.*"

"Because this is the *second* client of ours that's died this week."

He frowned. "It's not *our* fault we keep finding the bodies."

I called the police and they sent a few cars down. When Warner showed up, he was trailed by Robert. Who had called him? Robert looked down at the body on the ground and shook his head. "My God."

"Another suicide?" Warner asked.

"Murder," I said, pointing at the plastic bag of drugs on the carpet. "Heather didn't do drugs, and she sure as hell didn't kill herself. Just like Caroline didn't kill herself." I looked to Robert for some backup, but he was staring at the floor.

Warner pulled his mouth into a grim line. "How long did you know her, Sun?"

"A day," I said slowly. "What's your point?"

He raised one eyebrow. "So how could you know she wasn't a drug addict?"

Dean jumped in, "Because it doesn't take a genius to figure someone out. She was supposed to be meeting us today with some important information regarding the investigation. You don't find it odd that she winds up dead less than twelve hours later?"

140

Warner seemed peeved that he now had *two* sparring partners. "Maybe she was depressed. Her boss just died. You know, it's not uncommon for suicides to have a domino effect on relatives and friends."

"You can't be serious," I said, though he was *completely* serious.

"She *had* seemed off since she heard the news," Robert said, surprising me. What the hell? Was he buying this crap? Heather was the one who'd convinced him that Caroline's death wasn't an accident, and now he was going along with Warner's baloney?

"What do you mean? She was *fine* yesterday," I argued.

Warner shook his head. "After people make the decision to kill themselves they're usually on a high. They seem better, but it's just an illusion."

"*Yes, I know that*," I snapped. "That doesn't explain what happened here. Look around you," I gestured to the room. "This place is trashed. Someone was looking for something."

Warner glanced down at the body. "Maybe *she* was looking for something. Something she needed before taking her own life, a memento or keepsake."

My blood began to boil, and I could feel a flush creeping up my neck. I was going to punch this man in his stupid face if he swept this under the rug *again*.

Dean's hand moved to the small of my back. I looked over and he breathed in and out performatively, prompting me to do the same. I rolled my eyes and took in a breath before assessing the situation again. Warner was an ass—that wasn't news. Robert backpedaling was something I hadn't seen coming. He'd been so on board to find his wife's killer, what had changed?

"Have you been back to your house at all today?" I asked him.

He shook his head. "No, why?"

Dean said, "If someone was looking for something here they might have searched through your place as well."

Robert pulled out his phone and flicked through it. "No, everything looks fine." He held out his phone for us to see. He had one of those apps that monitored his security cameras. The house looked quiet, empty.

Hmm, well, there went that theory. Why would they trash Heather's place, but not look at Caroline's house first? Unless they *knew* they wouldn't find it there. Either because they'd already looked and come up empty, or because Caroline had hidden it somewhere else, and they knew that for a fact.

We left Warner and the police to do their investigation—not that they were going to do much, but maybe they'd get lucky. Out in the hall, Robert stopped us. "I know it was a short investigation, but I don't want you two poking around anymore."

Dean pinched his brows and was going to speak, but I placed a hand on his shoulder to stop him. "And why is that?" I asked, genuinely curious.

142

Robert's eyes went misty as he said, "I just can't handle it. I went along with Heather's theories because I was so upset yesterday. I wanted revenge. Now I realize the only person I could get revenge on is myself. It was *my* fault Caroline drank so much, *my* fault she'd made those stupid mistakes. And now Heather has followed in her footsteps? I can't accept this."

"Ending the investigation doesn't make either death a suicide," I said gently.

Robert shook his head. "The police are confident Caroline's death was an accident. A tragic accident. Heather was troubled and overworked. Maybe she didn't mean to kill herself. Most drug addicts don't."

I wanted to say more on the subject, although clearly there was no changing his mind, so I said instead, "Okay. We'll finish the paperwork and send over the invoice tomorrow morning for services rendered."

Robert nodded, his face long and looking much older than his fifty years. "Thank you. Both of you. I know you were hoping for something else, but it is what it is."

I nodded, shook his hand, and let him walk away.

Dean hit my shoulder and said, "What the hell? We're dropping the case?"

I rolled my eyes. "Of course not, dummy."

He pulled his brows together and bit his lip. "We're not? Then why did you say all that?"

I shook my head. "I don't know if Robert's judgment is just clouded by grief, or what's going on, but this case is far from over. He might not be paying us, but we have to get to the bottom of this. Two of our clients are dead."

Dean nodded, a fire in his eyes. "So what do we do now?" he asked.

"We need to find that boyfriend. Even if it turns out he's not the killer, he must know something important, maybe even where the will is."

"Do you think it's someone we've already interviewed?" Dean asked.

I nodded. "Oh definitely."

He looped his arm across my shoulders as we walked down the hallway. "Let's go find that sonofabitch, then."

ELEVEN

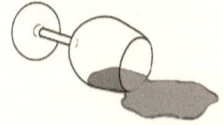

Dean tapped his pen against the edge of the notepad in thought. We were sitting in the Jeep in the parking lot behind the office. He'd written down the names of all the men we'd talk to already that were in Caroline's world. "Kirk is a no, right?" he asked. "I don't think he'd be cheating on his husband with a woman, especially one like Caroline."

I nodded. "I agree."

Dean crossed Kirk off the list. "And it's probably not Jake either, for the same reason. You know, because of the whole hot-guy-hidden-behind-the-partition thing."

"Agreed. I'm kinda surprised Caroline found any available straight men at a theater."

He scoffed. "Noah, there are tons of straight men in the theater world," Dean said, annoyed for some reason.

"Like?"

He waved his hand. "*Tim.*"

"Tim?" Timid Tim? We had seen him get a little loud, though maybe being quiet and submissive is what Caroline liked about him. "*Hmm*, maybe." Couldn't discount him yet.

"Harrison?" he asked.

I nodded. "Definite possibility, though again, why would they be fighting so much?"

Dean tapped his hand on the dash. "Unless it's all an act to keep the rest of the theater from finding out about them unlike Camilla and Robert.

I shrugged. "That could be true. It just seems so strange that both Caroline and Robert were having affairs right in front of the other."

"Happens all the time," he said matter-of-factly.

"Really? How would *you* know?"

Dean cocked his head to the side. "I may have been...involved in one or two."

I raised an eyebrow. "For a con?"

He smirked. "Sometimes, sometimes just because."

I shook my head. "Wow, you never cease to amaze me, Dean."

He grinned. "Thanks."

"That wasn't a compliment."

Dean ignored me. "Well, that's all the men we've talked to. Unless you think Caroline was taking a walk on the wild side."

"What?" I pinched my brows.

He gestured with his hands. "You know...lesbianism."

I cracked a smile. "I don't think so, Dean. Especially since Heather specifically said *boyfriend*."

He shrugged it off. "Whatever, let's keep it boring, I guess. So it's either Tim or Harrison."

"Why couldn't it be someone at her office?" I asked. "We haven't talked to anyone over there except for Heather."

"*Hmm*, if you think the theater world is gay you're going to have a fun time finding an available straight man at a fashion magazine."

I laughed. "I guess you're right."

"Plus whoever Caroline was seeing has to be connected with the theater, otherwise how would her blackmailer have found out about the two of them?" he said. "Most blackmailers don't follow people around, do they?"

"Sometimes," I said. "Usually only if they're professional blackmailers."

He raised his brows. "There are *professional* blackmailers?"

I nodded and blew out a breath. "Oh yeah, they usually have dozens or hundreds of people they're blackmailing at a time, who never find out who's targeting them. I doubt that's what's happening here, though."

"Agreed." Dean nodded. "Also the blackmail notes were on theater letterhead. Why would anyone at the magazine have access to that paper?"

"That's a fair point." I hadn't thought of that. It could be possible that someone was using the paper on purpose to throw us off? Probably not.

Dean paused for a second and then circled the two men's names. "So do we think that the blackmailer and the killer are the same person? Or two different people? I know we've sorta thrown around both ideas."

"*Hmm*, I don't know. Why would the blackmailer want to kill Caroline? That would be taking away their income."

"I know." Dean nodded. "I keep coming back to that will. Did someone kill Caroline because they'd been added to her will? Or did they kill her and *not* know about the will? Or *did* they know about the will, and maybe they wanted to kill her *before* it went into effect so that they could still inherit the money."

"You mean Robert?" I asked. "I assume that's who was named in her old will since she didn't write the new one until she found out Robert was cheating on her."

"But he has an alibi," Dean said. "As you keep reminding me."

I shrugged. "He could have hired someone? Rich people like doing that."

Dean flopped his arms at his side. "Great, so a random person? How would we ever find them? If he did hire someone they're probably a thousand miles away by now."

"I don't think Robert did it, I never have." I shook my head. "Didn't you see how he was today? He was totally broken up, on the verge of tears." Him firing us did catch me by surprise, but his judgment was obviously clouded by grief. He wasn't thinking clearly. Once we figured out who killed Caroline, he'd come around.

Dean frowned. "He owns a theater, Noah. He can probably act, he's a theater kid."

"*Hmm*, I don't think so." I just wasn't buying it.

"So where does that leave us?"

I groaned. "Let's just take things one step at a time and find out who this boyfriend is. That would solve one huge piece of the puzzle. Let's go find Tim. It's a long shot, but maybe it's him, or he can give us a better clue of who it could be. He was in Robert and Caroline's life every day, just as much as Heather was."

He pulled a hand through his hair, realized what he'd done, and looked in the visor mirror to fix his mistake. "I guess so. All this theorizing is getting us nowhere."

"Okay, Tim it is." I started the Jeep and pulled out of the lot.

* * *

"*So are we going to* break into his house or what?" Dean asked.

"What?" I furrowed my brow. "No, we're not going to be breaking into his house."

He frowned. "Why not?"

"Because that would be illegal, Dean."

Dean scoffed. "As if you've never done anything illegal before, Noah."

"That is beside the point," I mumbled.

He beamed and pointed a finger at me. "Ha, so you have."

"We're not breaking into his house," I said adamantly. "I'm not risking jail time for this case, sorry."

"*Hmm*, I might have another idea," Dean said.

I turned the corner. "I'm listening."

"Well nobody knows that Robert fired us, right? As far as everyone else is aware we're still on the case."

"*Yes?*" I said slowly.

"So we could go back to the theater and look through Tim's office, and nobody would think anything of it. Because we have permission to be there."

I shrugged. "I guess that's *technically* true. We'd have to do it before Robert got back, though. It would be really awkward if he caught us searching through his assistant's office. That is, if we can even get him away from his office in the first place.

"He might not even be there, but don't worry, I have a plan for that too," Dean said.

"Of course you do."

I parked the jeep in a public lot around the corner from the theater. I tugged at the collar of the pink striped suit. "I'm not wearing this anymore," I announced. "I have to change."

Deans shrugged. "Suit yourself."

"I, uh...don't have anywhere to change." My original clothes were in the back seat, but we were in a parking lot. Did the theater have a public bathroom?

Dean shook his head. "Just change right here, I won't look."

A blush crept up my neck. "No, that's a bad idea."

"Why?"

"Because!"

He smirked. "I'll close my eyes and look away, *promise*."

This was silly. I was turning this small moment into something bigger than it needed to be. "Fine." I grabbed my clothes from the back seat and peeled off the pink suit jacket, throwing it in Dean's lap. "Here, you can have that back."

"Careful," he admonished. "That's designer."

"*Whoopee.*" I started to unbutton the dress shirt until I got to about mid-chest and stopped.

Dean sighed and took the hint. "Oh, you were serious? Fine." He closed his eyes and placed his hands over his face. "Not looking."

I waved my hand in front of him to see if he'd react and then continued getting dressed. It was awkward to change in such a cramped space. I had to lean back and extend myself into the wheel well to pull the pink trousers off and slip my own dark chinos back on. When I was finally changed I cleared my throat. "I'm done."

"Are you sure?" Dean asked with a smirk. "I don't want to see something naughty and have my virtue sullied."

I rolled my eyes. "You are such a pill, Dean. Yes, I'm really done."

He opened his eyes and grinned, taking back the pink trousers and folding them along the crease line. "You're welcome."

"Thanks," I mumbled as I slipped out of the car.

When we walked around to the back door of the theater it was closed. "Damn, they always prop that stupid door open," I said. "Of all days to find it closed."

"It's fine," Dean said as he rapped his knuckles against the metal door. We waited for several minutes with no answer, so Dean knocked again. This time the door cracked open.

"What? We're not open to the public," Jake said in a dry tone.

"It's Detective Sun," I said as he opened the door wider.

He frowned. "Oh, it's you two again. Come to ask more questions?" He said it as if it was the last thing he wanted.

"Not to you, don't worry. Can we come in?" I asked.

He shrugged and opened the door for us. "Whatever."

"Thanks." We slipped past him into the hallway. I wondered what Jake was doing here so late in the afternoon. There didn't seem to be anyone else around for rehearsal. Maybe they were done for the day. Good. We'd miss Robert, then.

We made our way down the hall and up the stairs. No one else was around to stop us or protest our being there. "So what's your genius plan?" I asked as we scaled the spiral stairs.

"*Seduction*," he said slowly with a twinkle in his eye.

"Are you serious? I don't think you're Tim's type," I pointed out.

He shook his head. "No, not *that* kind of seduction, detective. We know that Tim has some sort of money problem, correct?"

"*Yeah*," I said, slowly understanding where he was going with this.

"And I am a former con man, ergo, I'm going to spin him an offer he can't possibly refuse."

"That seems unethical."

He rolled his eyes and frowned. "First we can't break into his house, now I can't con the man? What's next, we can't even talk to him?"

"Fine," I groaned. "But don't give him anything concrete, keep it really vague."

He grinned. "Trust me, I know what I'm doing, detective."

"I'll believe it when I see it," I said, just to annoy him.

"Wait at the end of the walkway, and I'll get him to follow me downstairs." He pointed down the catwalk.

I nodded and hid in the alcove at the end of the hall by the janitor's closet and the bathroom.

Dean sauntered down the catwalk and knocked on Tim's office door, all smiles and swagger. He slipped inside, and although I couldn't hear what he was saying, it clearly worked because a few minutes later Dean and Tim were walking back up the catwalk and down the spiral stairs.

That was easy enough.

I didn't have very much time to act, so I jogged down the walkway and slipped into Tim's office, closing the door behind me. The room was the same cramped, messy space from yesterday. What was I looking for? Some evidence of his affair with Caroline, or evidence that he was the blackmailer. There on the desk, was a stack of the same letterhead as the rest of the notes. It didn't necessarily mean anything, everyone had access to the same paper.

I shuffled through the paperwork on the desk, but it was all for the theater. There were notes about costumes, staging directions, printed out historical research, and stacks of playbills new and old. I started going through the drawers one by one, only it was more crap: pencils, notepads, candy bars, marketing fliers. The last drawer was more interesting—it was filled to the brim with old betting slips. Race horses, basketball games, car races, you name it. Now we finally knew why Tim was so desperate for money—he was a gambling addict. Did that make him desperate enough to kill? Maybe, maybe not, but it certainly made him a good suspect to be our blackmailer. On a wild hunch, I grabbed the stack of letterhead off the desk and craned my neck to get a better angle, to see the indents in the paper. Someone had written something recently. He couldn't have been stupid enough to write it on his own letterhead, could he?

I did the thing that I'd wanted to do since I became a detective, the thing everyone does in a PI story. I grabbed a pencil off the desk and started rubbing the lead gently against the last page of letterhead. Slowly, ghostly words began to appear on the paper.

Give me 5k or your husband knows all

"Oh my God, this guy really is dumb."

My phone buzzed in my pocket. Dean had texted me that they were coming back up, warning me to get out. Only I had the upper hand now, and I didn't plan on going anywhere. I waited a few minutes and then the door opened. Tim's eyes widened in surprise. "What are you doing in here?"

Dean, who was standing right behind Tim, raised an eyebrow, just as curious what I was up to.

"Really, *I* should be asking you that same question, Tim." I held up the page with its ominous message. "So when were you gonna tell us that you were blackmailing your boss's wife?"

Tim immediately deflated having been caught in a net. He crossed his arms and hunched inwards. "Please don't tell Robert, he'll fire me."

"Let's talk, shall we?" I moved to the side and let him sit down behind the desk. I showed the page to Dean, and he nodded, understanding. "So when did you start blackmailing Caroline?" I asked.

Tim shook his head. "About a month ago. But I need you to understand that I wasn't the first."

"What do you mean?" Dean asked.

He sighed. "I mean, I only started sending the notes after I heard about it from Heather."

"Someone had already been sending Caroline notes?" I asked.

He nodded. "She showed me one of the notes, how it was on official theater paper. She wanted to know if it was me, and obviously I told her no because it wasn't."

"*Yet*," Dean said.

Tim shrugged. "Exactly. I uh, needed some money, and I knew that Robert wouldn't give me a raise, even though I was owed one. I deserved one. So I took matters into my own hands. I mean, the money all kind of came from the same place anyway, so in a roundabout way I was actually blackmailing Robert, not Caroline."

That was a stretch.

"How long had Caroline been receiving notes before you decided to send your own?" I asked.

He shrugged. "I don't know, maybe another month?"

"That's probably why she stopped paying," Dean added, "when the notes started coming twice as often."

He was probably right. One note here and there was one thing, notes every week was another.

"Do you even know what Caroline was being blackmailed for?" I asked. Did he know about the boyfriend?

Tim shrugged. "I don't know, does it matter? She paid, that's all I cared about."

I laughed through my nose at his stupidity. "I see. And how much do you owe?" I asked, curiosity getting the better of me.

Tim shook his head. "What?"

"To your booky," I said. "I saw all the betting slips. There were hundreds of them."

"A lot," he finally replied. "A lot of money. More than I can repay."

I leaned over the desk. "So maybe when Robert refused to give you a raise and Caroline stopped paying your blackmail notes, you decided to do something about it?" I suggested.

"*What?*" His eyes widened. "No! I didn't have anything to do with what happened to Caroline. I swear. I gave you an alibi, remember? I was eating dinner with my parents, *nowhere* near the hills."

"*Hmm*, I guess I believe you," I said. "Did you ever figure out who the other blackmailer was?"

He shook his head. "No, but it must have been someone else at the theater, right?"

"Obviously." How else would they have the same letterhead?

Now that Tim was cornered and scared I figured there was no point in beating around the bush. Might as well go straight for the kill. "Were you sleeping with Caroline?" I asked.

His eyes went even wider, and he leaned back in his chair. "Of course not. What the hell kinda question is that?"

Dean shrugged. "We heard a rumor that you might have been seeing her behind Robert's back."

"Who the hell told you that?" he asked. "Because that's a bold-faced lie. I would never do that."

"But you *would* blackmail her?" I confirmed.

"That's not the same thing at all!"

I nodded. "Okay, well thanks for telling us."

Tim cleared his throat. "This isn't going to be in your report, right?" He wrung his hands together. "Robert can't know about any of this."

I shrugged casually. "We'll see." No reason to let him off *that* easily.

"What do you want from me?" he pleaded.

"What do you know about Harrison Black?" I asked. If the secret boyfriend wasn't Tim, Harrison was our next best suspect.

"Uh, I don't know him very well at all. He's good at what he does—we stole him from another theater uptown because of his skills. I don't really know anything personal about him, he kind of sticks to himself. I don't think he has much family or many friends."

"Any money problems?" I asked.

He jerked his head back and forth. "I don't know, I don't think so. Why? Do you think he was the other blackmailer?"

"We're keeping our options open," Dean replied.

Tim rubbed the back of his neck. "So, are we good?"

"For now," I said as I walked toward the door.

"Don't leave town," Dean said with narrowed eyes as we left and closed the door.

"You know only cops can say that, right?" I asked when we were far enough away.

He smirked. "I know. *He* doesn't know that, though. Besides, you did it yesterday!"

I rolled my eyes and smiled as we made our way downstairs and across the building to the lighting booth where we had found Harrison yesterday. Was he here?

Other than straight up asking him for the truth, we didn't have any evidence against him. We knew nothing about Caroline's boyfriend other than he existed, and even that we only knew because of Heather. Heather had said that she knew who it was, so why couldn't she have just texted it? Was she worried someone was going to find out? Who was close enough to Heather to even know she was talking to us? We'd told everyone that *Robert* was the one who'd hired us, not Heather. So why did they target her?

When we reached the control booth, the door was open and it was obviously empty. The cot was vacant, and the blanket was folded. Harrison was gone, and who knew when he'd be back.

"So what now?" Dean asked.

"I'm sure we can find out where Harrison lives," I said. "The problem is we don't have any leverage to use against him. He's defiant. If we try to strong-arm him he might not tell us anything we want to know."

Dean frowned. "And that leaves us where?"

"Maybe some of Caroline's employees knew about the boyfriend? She did say that they were a bunch of gossips when she first hired us."

He snapped his fingers and smiled. "That's a good idea. I mean, Caroline spent all her time at the magazine. We've been so focused on the theater because of the blackmailer, but Heather was one of dozens of employees that surrounded Caroline. Someone could know *something*."

I checked my watch. It was almost five. "We better go, people will start clocking out soon."

He nodded. "Right, give me the keys, and I'll go get the car started," he said in a rush.

160

He almost got me. I smiled. "Nice try. You're never driving my car, Dean. I've seen how you drive, and I'd like to keep my Jeep in one piece."

He sighed, his features sagging. "One of these days you're going to let me drive."

"And one of these days they're going to discover a new life form on the moon. *Anything is possible*," I said with a grin.

He narrowed his eyes. "You're so annoying."

I nudged his shoulder. "Right back atcha. Now come on, we're wasting time."

TWELVE

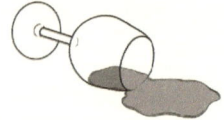

I drove across the city to downtown LA where Caroline's office was. Runway magazine was a fashion magazine founded in the eighties that focused on design trends and street style. Or at least that's what Dean explained to me as I drove. He was keyed into the fashion world. That was one of the reasons he'd stayed friends with Caroline for years even after deciding not to scam her.

"So it's a big deal?" I asked, out of the loop as usual. I didn't see why fashion was so important, or a billion dollar industry. A shirt was a shirt. Pants were pants. Who cared who made them?

"Yes, a *huge* deal. They're one of the top ten fashion magazines in the country, Noah."

"Oh."

"As much as her employees might gossip, I'm sure they had to be cutthroat and experienced to get a position at Runway. It's very competitive."

"So why has Fern never tried to get a job there?" I asked out of curiosity. "You already knew Caroline, wouldn't that have been perfect?"

He shook his head. "No, Fern would rather be *in* the magazine than writing the magazine. Not that she wouldn't be great at it."

"*Hmm.*" I pulled into the parking garage below the towering office building and took a ticket from the machine. Downtown LA was too damn expensive. I wondered if the magazine validated parking.

"I'll let you do most of the talking," I said as we got out of the car.

"Really?" Dean smiled, though he looked wary as if I might be kidding.

Dean was...good at people, better than me. Only, I didn't tell him that. I didn't want him to think I *needed* him or something. Because I didn't. It was just faster this way, and we were running out of time to solve the case now that Robert had fired us. "Yes, really. You've been here before, people probably remember you."

He smirked. "People *always* remember me."

"Good, then let's go." We took the elevator up to the top floor and entered the lobby for the magazine. Everything was blindingly white and shiny. It must have been a nightmare to clean.

Dean sauntered up to the bleached marble front desk and smiled at the receptionist. "Hi, Rebecca, right?"

The woman behind the counter had dark umber skin and long blonde braids up in a bun. She flashed a smile. "Right, and you're Dean? Caroline's friend?"

"Yes." Dean's face fell. "You heard about what happened?"

The woman sobered and nodded. "I'm *so* sorry. And then Heather too, it's unreal."

I was surprised the news of Heather's death had already spread since this morning. Had Robert told them?

Dean continued, "I know, it's terrible. I'm helping Robert put an event together this week in honor of Caroline, and I was wondering if I could walk around and talk to some of her employees, the people that knew her."

Rebecca nodded and said, "Of course, please," then she looked over at me.

Dean followed her gaze. "Oh, that's my event planner, Noah. He's just along for the ride."

I waved awkwardly.

"Well here, I'll give you both name tags so security doesn't give you any trouble. You remember where Caroline's office is, right?" she asked.

"Yeah, it's the corner office?" Dean said.

She nodded. "That's the one." She wrote out two name tags and handed them to us. "Let me know if you need anything else. It's been kinda crazy over here today, everyone is in a scramble. Especially after the cops came asking about Heather."

"They did?" I asked. That must be how they knew she was dead, not from Robert.

She nodded. "Yeah, they wanted to know if we thought she was unstable."

"And what did you say?" Dean asked.

She shook her head. "I told them no. I mean, Heather was wound up tight, but I never thought she was into drugs. She went out with us sometimes to a club or a bar, and she'd nurse one drink all night. She wasn't wild like that."

Dean nodded. "Yeah, I got that impression too. I hope they find out what happened. Anyway, thanks." Dean flashed his megawatt smile and motioned for me to follow him as we slipped past the front desk to the rest of the office. It was a fairly large space broken up into different quadrants.

"We should search her office too," I said quietly. "Maybe she left some clues on who this boyfriend might be."

"Isn't that *illegal*?" Dean asked, mocking me.

"Not if we have permission." I tapped my new name tag. "And we *have* permission."

He scoffed. "Yeah, okay."

We found her office easily. It was the biggest room in the building, all glass and steel. She had a large clear acrylic desk that was very neatly organized.

"I told you, Caroline was type A," Dean said. "I don't think we're going to find any hidden secrets just lying around here in a drawer. She wasn't Tim."

"We might be surprised." I checked out the notepads on the desk just out of curiosity, none were touched, practically fresh from the package. It almost looked like Caroline didn't even use her office as much as she had curated it. Who was responsible for that? Herself? Or Heather? She had an old-school Rolodex that I flipped through, secretly hoping she had a card labeled *secret boyfriend*, but no luck. The rest of the desk was unsurprising and unhelpful.

Dean started to look through the filing cabinet on the other side of the room. "This bottom drawer is locked," he said. "Could be promising?"

I walked over to check it out. "I didn't find a key anywhere. Do you think the receptionist would have one?"

"Don't bother." Dean pulled a small leather case out of his suit jacket pocket and plucked a metal pick from inside.

"You were just carrying that with you?" I asked. "In case we needed to break-in somewhere? I thought we talked about this, Dean. No more thievery."

He frowned. "It came in handy, didn't it? Besides, we haven't stolen anything...yet."

Predictably, the cabinet drawer was filled with hanging files, labeled in different colors. "*Ooh*, bills," Dean said.

"For the magazine?"

He shook his head. "No, better. For the theater." He stood up and handed me a small stack.

"Wow, Robert really wasn't thinking small, was he?" I said, pouring over the text. There were hundreds of charges adding up to tens of thousands of dollars. Anything from new lights to imported furnishings, handcrafted fabrics for costumes, and state-of-the-art sound systems. It was a complete overhaul for the theater and their production of The Marching Cry. "It looks like Caroline had her work cut out for her trying to slash these expenses. No wonder everyone was upset."

Dean scoffed. "It's Robert's fault for setting such high expectations that couldn't be met. Clearly the man has never heard of budgeting."

I thought that was funny coming from someone wearing a luxury bespoke suit.

I nodded. "And now I see why Caroline wanted proof of the cheating for the divorce lawyer. Otherwise Robert would've nickel-and-dimed every last penny out of her, the way he spends money."

"That brings up a great point," Dean said. "Do you think Robert knew that Caroline was also cheating on him?"

I shrugged. "Maybe not, maybe that's why she was so careful not to leave any traces for us to find."

He pinched his brows together. "*Hmm*, let's keep looking."

We snooped around for another few minutes without any luck. The bills for the theater were the only clue we found that really helped us.

"This place is way too clean," Dean said. "Let's hope some of these employees have loose lips like Caroline said they did."

"Have at it." I followed Dean into the open office space filled with more of the same—but smaller—acrylic desks. He found his first victim quickly—a petite blonde girl wearing lots of pink blush and a ruby red lip. I noticed that everyone in the office wore a lot of makeup and nice clothes. It *was* a fashion magazine, after all.

"Trisha, right?" Dean asked with a smile. They got to talking, and although she didn't know anything about who the secret boyfriend was, she'd heard a rumor that he existed. That rumor chain led us to a Chantrell, who led us to a Marcus, who led us to a Becky in marketing, and finally to Gigi—the social media editor for the magazine. Gigi was tall and leggy with long brown hair and dark eyes lined with charcoal.

"You saw Caroline with someone?" Dean asked.

She nodded and then looked around as if somebody was watching us. "Yeah, totally, and he *definitely* wasn't her husband."

"How could you tell?" I asked.

She cocked her head to the side. "Because Robert is kinda, like, pudgy, you know? And this guy was fit."

"Did you get a good look at him?" Dean asked.

She shook her head. "I saw them at the edge of the parking garage, like, a month ago. It was dark and hard to see, but I knew it must be a boyfriend because they were all touchy-feely. He kissed her, and then she got in his car."

"What kind of car?" I asked.

"*Hmm*, I don't know." She pinched her brows. "It was small, and like, dark."

Great details. I didn't bother asking if she saw the plate.

"Anything else you noticed about him?" I asked. "Was he tall? What color was his hair? How was he dressed?"

That seemed to catch her attention, and her eyes widened. "See, that's how I really knew it wasn't Robert, because Robert dresses all, bleh." Yes, she really said that. "And this guy was wearing nice trousers and a dress shirt. Very Prada, very chic. They looked like they were going on a date. And I only saw the back of him, but I think he had dark hair? Kinda short?"

A White guy with brown hair, that described half the men in LA—and more annoyingly, both of our suspects. Both Tim and Harrison could be characterized as tall and dark from far away. Though, I wouldn't say either would be considered *well dressed*. Tim was more middle-aged dad despite his youth, and Harrison dressed like a lazy rocker in band tees and ripped jeans. "Okay, thanks for the insight."

Gigi grinned. "Oh my God, I just gave a scoop to a detective. This is like that episode on NBC with Trip Traverty where he investigated a fashion magazine and it turned out the Chanel bags were *fakes*." She said *fakes* like it was the most disgusting word she could think of.

"Sure," Dean said. "It's exactly like that. Thanks again for your help."

We walked away quickly, distancing ourselves from any prying eyes and ears. "So does that help us?" Dean asked.

I shrugged. "A little? At least we have another eyewitness. We don't have to rely on the word of a dead woman that this boyfriend truly existed."

"You think that Heather would lie?" he asked.

I shook my head. "No, I don't, but we also don't really have much evidence to support the idea yet. Let's go back to the office and sort through this crapshoot, then maybe we can find out where Harrison lives and try and get something out of him, with or without evidence."

"Okay."

We rode the elevator down to the parking garage and stepped out. The late afternoon sun was harsh, making the underground garage dark and shadowy in contrast. Dean held up his hand in front of my face, a keychain of keys looped around his finger. "Gotcha."

I was confused for a moment until I patted my trouser pocket and felt it empty. "Very funny, you're still not driving the Jeep." I reached out for the keys, only Dean had already begun to jog away. I ran to catch up to him. "Come on, Dean, this is ridiculous."

Squeal. Tires against asphalt.

A dark sedan zoomed across the garage, aiming straight for Dean. In a split-second of panic I dived and pulled Dean to the ground behind a cement column. Crashing onto the pavement was so disorienting I hardly caught a look at the car as it *smashed* through the plastic ticket gate and peeled out of the garage.

"Dammit." My heart thundered in my chest as I tried to catch my breath. Below me, Dean's eyes were wide, and he was speechless—for once. I was inadvertently laying on top of his solid chest.

It only took him a moment to regain his composure again. "Are you wearing the cologne I got you?"

I huffed out a dizzy laugh. "We almost got made into roadkill, and that's what you're asking me?"

He smiled. "You are, aren't you? It smells good."

With an eye roll I heaved myself off of him and stood up. The knees of my chinos were shredded, as well as my palms. "Are you okay?" I pulled him to his feet and he sucked in a breath through his teeth, his brow furrowing.

"I think I tweaked my knee when you pushed me out of the way," he said.

"I'm sorry." I knelt down to inspect the damage. His suit was more or less fine, only a scuff on his elbow where he'd hit the ground and a scratch or two on his legs.

I felt his knee with my palm, and he sucked in a sharp breath. "*Ow*, stop touching it!"

"Okay, let's get you to the ER," I said as I pulled him to a standing position.

He shook his head. "I'm fine."

"No, you're *not* fine. Come on. We need to get out of here anyway. What happens if our killer comes back to inspect his handiwork?"

"Shit."

"Yeah, lean on me." I looped my arm around his shoulders and we hobbled over to the Jeep on the other side of the parking garage. "Did you see the car?" I asked. "I didn't get a good look at it."

He shook his head. "No, and I'm usually pretty good with cars. Looked like a late nineties sedan of some sort. Hard to tell. Maybe a Lincoln?"

I nodded. "Okay." I helped him into the passenger seat, and then after taking quick stock of myself, I drove him to the hospital.

We hung around in the waiting room for over an hour before they could see Dean. He had both an x-ray and an examination from the doctor. They determined that nothing was broken or torn, just badly twisted. They prescribed a knee brace and a Tylenol.

"Fat lot of good that was," Dean said as we were leaving. "I told you we should have just gone home."

"You got a fancy brace, didn't you?" I said as I helped him back to the car.

"Yeah and it totally clashes with this suit."

The black brace on top of his gray and pink pinstripe looked fine to me. I rolled my eyes. "Because that's what we should be focusing on. You're right, Dean. Not the fact that someone just tried to kill us...again."

"So apparently we're getting close?" he said. "I don't feel very close."

I shook my head. "Neither do I. Let's go call our families."

He cringed. "Fern is *not* going to be happy I almost got killed again."

"Neither is Lexi," I said. "But it comes with the trade—pissing people off."

"Yeah, but who?" he exclaimed. "The killer? The boyfriend? The other blackmailer? You don't think Tim was ballsy enough to kill us just so we wouldn't tattletale on him to Robert, do you?"

"*Hmm*, I don't think so." I shook my head and crossed my arms. "You saw how he cowered when I threatened him earlier. He might have gotten loud with Robert during that argument, but I don't think he has the gall to kill someone, even if he is desperate." I helped Dean into the Jeep and we drove back across the city to the office.

Lexi met us in the alley behind the building, her arms crossed and her face set in a scowl.

"What?" I asked as I opened the car door.

"I told you to stop getting hurt," she said. "Why didn't you listen?"

"It's not like I was *trying* to get run over." I jogged to the other side of the car, and Dean leaned on me as he stood up.

"And you," she said, pointing straight at Dean. "You promised to keep my uncle out of trouble."

He grinned a goofy smile. "I don't remember making that promise."

She scoffed. "Well you did."

"Where's Captain?" I asked. Captain usually greeted me when I came home whenever Lexi was watching him for me.

She narrowed her eyes. "I let him into the office so he could pee on your desk chair as punishment."

I raised my brows. "Diabolical."

She smiled, "Thanks," then remembered she was supposed to be mad and scowled again. "Don't try to be cute, Uncle Noah. What would I do if you got yourself killed? I'd be stuck with my parents and Grandma all the time."

I shrugged. "They're not *all* bad."

"That's beside the point. Come on, you two. You better get inside before someone else tries to kill you."

Lexi grabbed Dean's other arm and we hobbled through the back door. It took a minute to get up the stairs, but eventually we made it to the office. Dean collapsed in the old office couch that sat in the small seating area just inside the space. Malcolm and I had found the couch on the side of the road one day and added it to our mishmashed collection of thrift store furniture and hand-me-downs.

"I'm beat," Dean said.

I chuckled. "More like beat up."

Dean winced in pain as he scooted across the sofa cushion so he could lay down.

"I'm gonna get some ice," Lexi said and walked out of the office in the direction of my apartment.

"That's a good idea."

It was quiet for a second. I didn't want to sit despite how tired I was, so I crouched down by the sofa. "You scared me," I said.

Dean laughed. "I scared *you*? You scared *me*! You tackled me like a linebacker."

I smiled. "Do you even know what a linebacker is?"

He frowned. "Yeah, totally, they're the big one that...backs the line, or whatever. It's not important, Noah."

I shook my head and chuckled. "No, of course not."

"Last time you broke my fall," Dean said. "This time it was me. I guess now we're even."

I nodded. "I was hoping we *wouldn't* almost get murdered again, but I suppose you're right."

"Thanks for saving me," he said.

"Thanks for not dying."

He cracked a smile. "You're welcome."

The space between us was tense. My chest was tight, and my heart fluttered.

Dean stared at me, his dark eyes piercing mine.

"Here's that ice pack," Lexi said as she came back with the frozen gel pad.

I hopped up and took the other seat across from the couch as Lexi placed the ice pack under Dean's knee. If she noticed the awkward energy she didn't show it.

Dean grinned. "Thanks." Lexi flicked him in the forehead making him scowl. "Ow! What the hell?"

"*Don't get hurt,*" Lexi admonished. "How complicated is that?"

"I'll try harder next time," he said, rubbing his forehead.

She smiled and laughed through her nose. "You better."

THIRTEEN

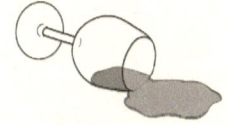

"What happened?" Fern asked as she walked through the door. Dean had been careful to give her as little information as possible over the phone. Of course, she'd dropped everything and had driven over to the office.

"How was the shoot, darling?" Dean asked with his go-to smile.

Fern frowned. "Don't deflect. Did you get in a fight?" She crouched down to the carpet and inspected his knee brace. "Or worse?" She was dressed in a pale pink silk dress with some kind of flower design. Her usually curly golden locks were up in a tight updo.

"It was nothing," Dean insisted.

"They almost got run over by some psycho," Lexi confessed.

Fern gasped dramatically. "Someone tried to kill you on purpose? *Again?*"

I raised my hand. "I heroically pushed him out of harm's way." I could see the murderous look behind her eyes, and I was determined not to let it land on me.

"Not very heroic if he injured his knee," she said with her lips in a flat, unamused line.

"Better than dead?" I offered.

"Let's get back on track," Lexi said. "You two seem to have a lot of random, jumbled information, and we need to sort it out into something that makes a little more sense."

That was Lexi, always business.

"You're right." I pulled out my notepad, and Lexi opened her laptop. She sat down in one of the chairs next to me while Fern sat on the couch beside Dean, resting his head on her lap. She pet his forehead and ran her fingers through his dark locks. At first, when I'd met the pair weeks ago I'd assumed they were a couple by how much they obviously cared for each other. Turned out they were more like brother and sister than anything else. They were all the other had in the world. I didn't know much about Fern's background, but Dean had told me both his parents were dead, and that he had nobody else, at least no one that he wanted to be around. I hadn't pushed for details.

"So, how do we sort this mess?" Dean asked from the couch.

"We need some lists, some pros and cons," I said.

Lexi started typing. "On it."

We ran through all the names of the people we'd interviewed the last two days along with their alibis—some good, some bad.

"What about Jake's alibi, did you check that out?" Dean asked.

I nodded. "Yeah I called his understudy yesterday, and he said that Jake was at the club with a large group of castmates during the time of the murder. They didn't get home until late in the morning. I also talked to Kirk's husband and Christina's boyfriend. They both confirmed their respective alibis."

"And Tim?" Dean asked.

"Funny you mention that." I laughed through my nose. "You know how he said that he was at his parents' house all night?"

Dean raised a brow. "Yeah?"

"Well, that was only half the truth. He *was* at his parents' place for dinner, but afterwards he was at a local casino until the early morning. Security confirmed that he was there at the time of the murder. Apparently, he's a regular. I mean, maybe he could have slipped out and snuck back in, but it's hard to say."

Dean's eyes went wide. "Wow."

"But Tim *was* the blackmailer?" Lexi confirmed.

I shook my head. "Only *one* of them. He only started writing notes after hearing about the first blackmailer, so that's still up in the air. I don't

179

think the blackmailer had anything to do with the murder, though. I really don't. Heather presented it as one of her arguments why she thought Caroline was murdered, but I don't see how they're connected. Why would her blackmailer kill her and end their cash flow? That's what I keep coming back to."

"So do you think that clears Tim?" Lexi asked.

I nodded. "I think so. We talked about it earlier. He doesn't have the nerve to pull something like that off. Plus, we know he didn't kill Heather. He was at the theater all morning, which was confirmed by other staff members there at the time."

Lexi typed that down. "Okay."

"What about Harrison?" Dean asked.

I raised an eyebrow. "For the boyfriend?"

He nodded.

"I can see it, but if he *was* the boyfriend, then why kill Caroline?" I asked.

Fern jumped in, "Maybe the affair was just a means to an end?"

"Yes, the will," Dean said. "It all comes back to that will."

"It *could* work, the timeline is right," I said. "Caroline made the new will just after starting her affair and learning about Robert and Camilla. She probably hadn't known this boyfriend for very long, and she made a rash decision." I held up a hand. "Though, we don't actually know for certain that the boyfriend was added to the will, we're just assuming that's the case."

"You couldn't get a copy?" Fern asked.

I shook my head. "Nope, the lawyers are holding it close to their chest, and whatever copy Caroline had, someone else—the killer—is still looking for it. They didn't find the will at Heather's place."

Dean jumped in from the couch, "So the way we see it now is that either Robert killed her, hoping to cash in the money before the new will went into effect, or this new boyfriend killed her for the opposite reason. Only Robert has an alibi, so if it was him, he must have hired somebody to kill Caroline for him."

Lexi scrunched up her nose. "That doesn't make sense with what we know of the murder, though, right? Caroline knew someone was coming over which is why she put the dog upstairs, something she rarely did, and the doors were untampered. She let her killer inside. That fits with the boyfriend angle."

I nodded. "I agree. Dean seems to have something against Robert."

Dean frowned and pinched his brows. "I do not. You just don't see his sinister nature like I do. It's in the eyes."

Fern patted his shoulder.

"I think that logic makes sense," Lexi said. "That the boyfriend manipulated Caroline into adding him to her will and then killed her for the money."

"But won't that information come out soon?" Fern asked. "Whoever inherits the money had to have been the killer."

I scoffed. "If the police actually wanted to investigate, maybe. They're still stuck at step one where they think this was all just a tragic accident."

"Even after the death of that girl, Heather?" Fern asked, surprised.

"Yep." I nodded. "I think Warner makes dumb decisions just to spite me sometimes, I really do."

"So whoever gets the money can just cut and run without anyone finding out?" Fern asked. "That's crazy."

I agreed. "Which is why we need to figure this out sooner rather than later. Whoever is looking for that will knows their name is on it and wants to stop anyone else from finding out, or they want to *make sure* their name is on it. Either way, they're desperate, and desperation makes people do crazy things."

"Clearly," Dean said. "We must be getting a little too close for their comfort if they feel the need to get rid of us."

"They're starting to make stupid mistakes. That's good," I said. "We got them right where we want them. We just have to figure out who's lying."

Lexi typed something down onto her computer. "So, as far as we know, both Robert and Camilla are out for the murder."

I nodded. "Yep, obviously Heather as well. That was a theory being thrown around by Harrison and Camilla. I wouldn't be surprised if Warner went for that angle next: that Heather killed Caroline and felt so guilty she then killed herself. But that would be insane. *Someone* searched her apartment for that will. *Someone* just tried to mow us down. We know it wasn't Heather.

Lexi nodded and kept typing. "Tim, out?" she asked with a raised brow.

"Yes," I agreed.

Dean nodded. "And we know the boyfriend was a man, obviously, so we can safely cut out both the women at the theater—Gwen and Christina. Gwen's alibi wasn't the best, but she seemed to be the only one at the theater who was on good terms with Caroline. They could both still be our second blackmailer, though. With how this case is going, you never know."

"Okay, so no women," Lexi said. "That just leaves Kirk, Jake, and Harrison in the suspect pool."

Dean shook his head. "Both Jake and Kirk are gay. So they couldn't be the secret boyfriend. That just leaves one man—Harrison. He has no good alibi, he let everyone know he hated Caroline, and he needed the money for the theater. He was complaining to us how Caroline wanted to slash his lighting budget, and he wasn't happy about it."

"Let's get on that alibi, then," I said. I flipped through my notepad and found the number for Harrison's so-called *friend* who was his alibi for that night. I called the number and waited for someone to answer.

"Hello?" a lazy, deep voice said.

"Hey, is this Harrison's friend?" I asked.

He hesitated and then said, "Maybe, does he owe you money?"

"Nah, nothing like that." I didn't want to tip him off that Harrison might be in trouble, but it was possible that he had already told his friend about me, and this guy knew exactly who I was. "I just need to know where Harrison was on Friday night?"

"Why do you want to know?"

I sighed and channeled my inner Dean, weaving a story together. "My girl used to date Harrison. She was gone all Friday night, and she said she was out with her girlfriends, but man, I don't know. I just want to make sure she wasn't lying to me."

That seemed to make him relax. "Ha, sounds like Harrison, but you're in the clear, man. We were at McTavish's that night. We watched the band play for a while, but Harris got sloshed before they even finished, so I helped him get home a bit early before the puking started. He wasn't with any girl."

I let out a deep breath. "Good, so you were with him the whole night?"

He hesitated. "Nah, I mean, I took him home around ten, tucked him in bed and all that shit. I left him there. But he was in no state to be seeing any girl, trust me. You're good, bro."

"*Hmm*, thanks, man. I appreciate it."

He paused. "Hey, how'd you get my number by the way?"

I hung up without answering the question. I'd gotten everything I could from him.

Dean started clapping slowly. "Bravo, Noah. Enthralling performance."

I rolled my eyes, but couldn't help but smile. "So Harrison's alibi is useless. He was home alone during the time of the murder which was around or after eleven."

"He's our guy," Dean agreed.

I shrugged. "Now comes the trouble of proving it."

"So if you think this Harrison guy is the killer, does that mean he was also the blackmailer?" Fern asked.

I shook my head. "He says that he wasn't, and surprisingly he was also the one who told us about the will in the first place," I said. "Maybe it was deflection? Either way it was a reckless move. "

"I don't suppose you can match the handwriting on the notes, can you?" Lexi asked.

I hadn't thought of that, but it wouldn't be any good. "The handwriting was masked with blocky font. And Tim copied the same weird script, so nobody even realized there were two blackmailers until we caught him."

Lexi deflated. "Oh, so that wouldn't help? Is Harrison right-handed?"

I shook my head. "I don't remember. Dean?"

He cocked his head in thought. "Actually, you're right. He *was* left-handed. He wrote down the name of his buddy, remember?"

I looked down at the notepad and Lexi leaned over to point at the text. "See how it slants slightly to the left? That's a telltale sign. Do you have the blackmail notes?"

I grabbed the case file from my office and came back with the notes. They all looked the same at first glance, all written on the same letterhead in the same basic black ink. Every single one had the blocky font I'd described.

"I can't tell." I spread out the pages on the coffee table between us, and Lexi knelt down to the carpet to examine them closer.

"See? This one." She pointed to the page. "See how the A slants slightly to the right? This must have been Tim's note."

I nodded. "That tracks. The note is asking for four thousand. The numbers increased with every note, so it must have been one of the last notes before Caroline got fed up and decided to stop playing the game."

"But this one." She picked up a page. "The first letter slants to the left."

Damn, she was right. The G in *give* was crooked.

"Is anyone else in your suspect pool left-handed?" Fern asked. "It could be a coincidence."

A valid point. "I have no idea. We weren't thinking about it at the time."

Dean raised his head. "But everything else lines up. Everything points to Harrison. Now we even have a handwriting sample to match it to." He gestured at my notepad.

No, it was too hard to say. The blocky letters didn't look anything like Harrison's scribbled font, but that was the point. It was *supposed* to be unrecognizable.

We didn't have much evidence, but if no one else was left-handed, Harrison was our best guess at our second blackmailer. He was also our best suspect for Caroline's secret boyfriend.

"But now we have a problem," I said.

"What now?" Dean whined from the couch, gazing up at the ceiling.

"If Harrison is the second blackmailer, why would he kill Caroline?" I said. "We already discussed that the blackmailer would want to keep Caroline alive for more money so..."

"But she'd stopped paying," Lexi pointed out. "And if he knew that Caroline had added him to her will for a fact, he had the perfect opportunity to make some *real* money. He didn't need to blackmail her anymore. Why con her for small sums of money when he could have the whole pot?"

I nodded reluctantly. "I suppose you're right. That could make sense. Especially if money was his only motive."

"Exactly," Dean agreed.

"But I don't think Harrison being left-handed is enough evidence to prove anything," I said. "So we need to figure out another angle. If he left his apartment on Friday night after his friend dropped him off then maybe someone saw him?"

"How would we find that out?" Dean asked. "The security cameras at Caroline's place were conveniently off, and that means we don't have any footage from the house."

I scratched my chin. "No, but maybe we can get footage from somewhere near Harrison's apartment?" We weren't cops, we didn't have access to traffic cameras, but if there was a business next to Harrison's apartment it was possible we could catch his car on those cameras. Speaking of that. "We also need to find out what kind of car Harrison drives. Maybe he was stupid enough to try and kill us with his own car."

"Okay, well let's go," Dean said, trying to rise from the couch.

Fern frowned and pushed him back down. "I think not. You're injured, Dean."

"I'll go," I said, standing up. "It shouldn't take me long, and I can check on the car angle at the same time."

"Can I come?" Lexi asked, hopping up from her seat.

I raised an eyebrow. "Where do your parents think you are right now?"

"Korean club," she confessed, her shoulders drooping.

I crossed my arms. "I'll drop you off at home. There's no way I'm taking you to the residence of a potential murderer, Lexi. Give me *some* credit."

"What's the big deal?" She rolled her eyes. "It's just an apartment, it's not as if he's gonna murder us."

I scoffed. "That's what *you* think, he might have other plans."

Dean sighed. "And I guess I'll just be here, then."

I nodded and said in a chipper tone, "Sounds good to me."

Fern patted his chest. "You need to rest, darling. No more of this running around and getting yourself killed."

Dean frowned and pinched his brows. "I'm not a baby."

I grinned and leaned over to smush his cheeks together. "Baby can take a nap while the *real* detective does some *real* detective work."

He narrowed his eyes. "That's it, I'm definitely *not* getting you that *best boss* mug I had my eye on."

I shrugged. "Good, because Lexi already got me that one last year."

Lexi scoffed. "I did *not*."

"Uh, yeah, you did. Have the mug to prove it."

She rolled her eyes and stayed silent.

"I'll be back soon, get some rest," I said. "Make sure to lock the doors after I leave."

Dean scowled. "I'll be sure to do that, detective."

With a final smile, I left the office with Lexi trailing behind. We got in the Jeep and I drove her home, down to the south side of LA. She let out a deep breath of teen angst as I parked in her driveway. "Are you sure you don't need me?" she asked, pleading in her eyes.

I smiled. "I always need you, kid, just not right now. Besides, your dad would *literally* kill me if he knew I'd brought you to the home of a suspected killer."

She shook her head, the corner of her lips turning up in a smile. "Whatever, he'd get over it."

I scoffed. "Yeah, a couple years after I've been in the grave, *maybe*."

"Bye, Uncle Noah. Go catch some bad guys for me," she said as she slipped out of the car.

"Will do." I waved as she retreated into the house. I was about to back out of the driveway when the door opened again, and my mother walked down the path. What was she doing here?

I rolled down my window reluctantly. "Hi, Mom."

She smiled, though her eyebrows were drawn. "Hi, Noah. I see you picked Lexi up from Korean club?"

I nodded. "Yep, Korean club," I lied. It was dark outside, the streetlights already turning on. It was pretty late for a school club. If she saw through the lie, she didn't say anything.

"You haven't been texting me back," she said. It wasn't a question, it was an accusation.

Crap. "Uh, yeah, I've just been really swamped with this new case I told you about. Sorry."

"I see." She crossed her arms. "Lexi tells me that you hired a new partner?"

Oh, so *that's* what this was about.

"Yeah, I did."

She pinched her brows. "And you can afford that?"

Not really, at least not right now. "Yes, of course. I'm fine, Mom."

I could tell under her rigid exterior she was worried about me. "Well if you say so."

I nodded. "I do."

She shifted her weight. "Well, when do we get to meet this man?"

I laughed through my nose. "I don't know. Do you *need* to meet him?" Why was she acting like Dean was some boyfriend I'd been hiding from her?

She scoffed. "Well of course I do. He's important to your business, and therefore he's important to me."

I raised an eyebrow. Since when did she care about my business? My parents had been hounding me to shut the place down since the minute I opened the agency. "Okay. You can meet him soon. It won't be until after this case is closed. We're on a time crunch. Speaking of that, I kinda gotta go, Mom."

She sighed. "Of course you do. Well, be safe. You know how I worry."

"I know." She wouldn't let me forget it.

She leaned into the car and kissed my cheek. "Text me, okay?"

"Okay, Mom."

I pulled out of the driveway and onto the road. I hadn't realized my parents even knew about Dean. Not that it was some kind of secret. I hadn't instructed Lexi not to tell them. They wanted to meet him. For some odd reason I couldn't place, the idea made me nervous. What if they didn't like Dean? Or worse, what if they *did*? I felt the need to protect him from them. What was that? We weren't dating, and he annoyed me so much we were hardly friends. And yet, he was also one of the closest people in my life even though I'd only known him less than a month.

I'd have to bring up the idea to Dean later. No doubt, he'd have a field day with that one.

After putting the issue at the back of my mind I drove over to Harrison's apartment. It was on the edge of Hollywood near the south side, so not too far from my brother's house. I'd gotten the address from Tim, who when I texted, was more than eager to give me whatever I wanted in exchange for keeping my mouth shut about the whole scamming his boss's wife thing.

When I arrived, I was annoyed to find out that it was more suburban than I'd hoped. No businesses meant no cameras. Harrison's apartment was a mid-rise building surrounded by a block of single-family homes. Not what I'd expected for a grungy artsy type like Harrison. I thought he'd live in some hipster warehouse apartment near a more urban district of LA.

I parallel parked across the street and got out. The apartment building was small with limited parking spots in the lot. I searched the painted pavement for the number of Harrison's apartment. It was dark with limited lighting, so it took me a minute of squinting and squatting. Number twelve. *Bingo.* In the spot sat a dark green Subaru from the early 2000s. Not the black sedan that had tried to run us over a few hours ago. That didn't necessarily mean that Harrison wasn't our guy. It just meant that he wasn't stupid enough to use his own car in his attempted manslaughter. Tack that one on to his list of crimes.

Feeling discouraged, I was about to leave, when something caught my eye. The house across the street was clearly from the sixties and had about a dozen standing birdhouses and bird feeders littering the front yard. But what had caught my attention was the glint from a camera lens attached to the post in front of the porch. A *video* camera. What were the chances that the camera had a view of this side of the street?

I walked over and knocked on the door. I had nothing to lose. I found myself wishing that Dean was here for this part and almost laughed. A couple weeks ago I couldn't wait to get him out of my hair, but now I was wishing he could do his social butterfly routine and get me some answers.

The door cracked open, and an old woman with thick coke-bottle glasses and a puff of permed white hair appeared. "Yes?"

"Are you an avid bird watcher?" I asked, trying to start with her interests instead of asking for what I wanted. That seemed like something that Dean would do.

She raised one eyebrow. "Yes, I am. Why do you ask?"

I explained who I was. "I'm trying to see when someone across the street from you got home on Friday night. Does your camera," I pointed to the camera, "capture that angle, or is it just the birds?"

She seemed to relax, her expression melting into an open smile. "Well it's funny you should mention that, because some kids were messing with my setup the other day, and they moved the camera around. I don't know what you're looking for, but you might as well come inside and take a gander."

I grinned. "Thanks."

I wandered into the house. The living room was like a time capsule straight from the sixties, including the plastic covered floral sofa.

"I'm not too good at all this technology stuff, but my grandson bought me that camera this year so I could catch the hummingbirds in the mornings." She sat down at a desk with a massive, decades-old PC computer. "He said the camera was wireless, so I guess the video gets automatically downloaded here. I don't know. You have a look-see and tell me what you think." She got up and traded places with me.

"Thank you." The desktop was busy with folders in a random arrangement. It took me a minute to find the folder for the camera footage. It was labeled a random string of numbers, most likely the serial number for the camera. Inside the folder were dozens of clips, date stamped. I found the video for Friday and let out a prayer. I clicked on the video and waited for the old computer to load the graphics. The camera was pointed at the birdhouses, but you could *just* see the driveway for the apartment building across the street in the corner. It was blurry, since the bird feeders were in the foreground, but it was still good enough to see.

I scrolled through the timeline until Harrison's friend dropped him off around ten o'clock. "There." A red car pulled into the lot and two figures emerged, one holding the other up. So his friend hadn't been lying about that part at least. Let's see if Harrison stayed put like he said. I played the video in real time, watching the minutes tick by. It was past ten thirty and dark—luckily the apartment was lit up along with the small suburban street. It wasn't great footage, barely good enough to see.

10:37. Harrison's green Subaru pulled out of the lot and onto the road. My heartbeat picked up. "Got him." He was a liar, and now we had proof. The trouble was going to be, how to use it?

Tabby—I'd learned was her name—let me download the video onto my phone. "Thank you so much. You've been very helpful."

She smiled. "I'm glad. This neighborhood used to be very quiet and tranquil before all those apartments moved in and people started running amuck. I'm happy someone is still trying to safeguard our community."

I didn't know about all that, but I smiled and nodded genially anyway.

Now that we had something to use against Harrison, we were one step closer to proving he killed Caroline.

FOURTEEN

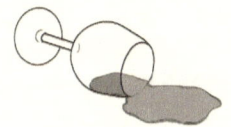

I was halfway between Harrison's apartment and the office when my phone began to ring. It was an unknown number. *Hmm.* I answered the call and said, "Hello, Detective Sun speaking."

There was heavy breathing over the line, nervous breathing. "Yes, detective, this is Kirk Landry from the theater," he said.

"I remember. What's up, Kirk?" Why was he calling *me* of all people?

"I uh, I need to talk to you," he said.

I nodded. "Hence the phone call. What's going on?"

"No, no, in *person*," he said, his voice taking on a hard edge. "It *has* to be in person."

"Why?" His whole attitude had changed since the first time I'd met him.

He paused and then said quietly, "What I have to tell you could change *everything*."

Very helpful. "In what way?"

"I can't say more. Will you meet me? At the theater?"

"Now?" I asked.

"*Yes*," he barked. "*Yes*, now. I'm afraid for my life, detective. I can't keep this secret any longer."

"Okay, okay, hang tight. I'll be right over."

He breathed a sigh of relief. "Thank you, detective. I'll be hiding in the costume department. Come find me."

"Okay." I hung up the phone and hightailed it across town back to Hollywood and back to the Hydecker Theater. The street was busy with early nightlife, but the building itself looked dark and quiet. Rehearsals had to have been finished for the night. I parked and entered the building through the back door. If Kirk was trying to protect himself, this open entrance probably wasn't the best idea. The last time we'd talked to Kirk had been outside, so finding the costume department again was going to be an undertaking.

I followed the lit hallway, reading signs above doors as I passed dressing rooms and the makeup department. I turned down a second hallway to the left and found a set of doors marked *costumes*. Finally. I knocked.

There was a startled yip on the other side of the door. "It's just me. Detective Sun," I said.

"Oh thank God," Kirk said, "I thought you were him."

"Him?"

He ignored my question. "If I had known it would turn out like this I would've never blackmailed her."

"You were the one blackmailing Caroline?" I thought back to the fancy clothes and the gold watch. I'd thought Kirk was just doing well for himself. Now it made more sense. "Can you open the door?' I asked. It was silly talking through a wooden door.

"Hang on, I blocked the entrance with a heavy vanity," he said. "I didn't want anyone getting in."

I shook my head. *Smart move.* "Why are you worried someone is coming to hurt you?" I asked. There was a scraping sound and then lots of shuffling.

"Because! Heather is dead, and when I got here earlier the costume department and the prop department had both been ransacked. There's stuff everywhere back here!"

So whoever had killed Caroline was still looking for the will, and by Kirk's own admission, it wasn't the blackmailer who was doing it. It had to be the boyfriend. So the boyfriend was, without a doubt, the killer.

More scraping, more scuffling.

"Who was Caroline dating?" I asked. "Was it Harrison?"

I received a scream in reply.

"Kirk?"

"*No, no, please!*" he cried out.

I banged up against the door. It was locked, and there was still something heavy wedged up against it. "Kirk?" I shoved the door again with my shoulder. It wasn't budging.

He'd gone silent. Then there was more scuffling, but it was muffled. "Kirk!"

There had to be a second entrance to that room. How else could Kirk have been attacked? Was he dead?

I raced down the hall and turned the corner. This place was a maze. Two more turns and I found an unmarked door that seemed to be in the right place. It was unlocked. Just as I turned the knob to enter, a body smashed into me, knocking me to the floor. I caught a brief glance at the intruder—average height, average weight, square in all the ways that a man would be. He was wearing a dark hoodie that covered his face. Damn.

I thought about chasing after him, but Kirk was more important. I jumped up from the ground and rushed inside the costume department. It really was a mess. Clothes were thrown everywhere, shelves were either ransacked or tipped over, and there were hangers and small objects littering the floor. Did they think the will was hidden inside a costume? How savvy did they think Caroline was?

"Kirk?" I ran towards the opposite corner past rows and rows of overturned costumes. Kirk was splayed on the floor. There was no blood. "Kirk?" I asked again as I reached him and knelt down to the carpet. I placed my fingers on his neck. He had a pulse. He wasn't dead, just unconscious. There was a heavy prop statue lying on the floor beside him. Someone must have hit him in the head during the struggle.

Again someone had gotten to a witness just as they were going to tell me the identity of the unknown boyfriend. If it wasn't tragic it would be funny.

I called the paramedics and they took Kirk down to the hospital where the cops then met us to take my statement. Kirk still hadn't woken up by the time Dean called me an hour later. I filled him in on everything that had happened.

"Damn. *Kirk* was the other blackmailer? So it had nothing to do with the murder or the boyfriend?"

I bit my lip absentmindedly. "Apparently not. He just saw an opportunity and took it."

"And he didn't say who the boyfriend was?" Dean confirmed.

I shook my head. "No, unfortunately we got interrupted. I'll give you one guess, though." I told Dean what I'd learned from the bird lady's video footage.

Dean took in a sharp breath. "So Harrison *doesn't* have an alibi, *and* he left his house just before Caroline's murder?"

"*Uh-huh.*"

"So it's gotta be Harrison, right?" Dean asked. "He lied for no reason, and everything else points to him."

"Looks like it. And now we have proof, so we can pressure him into revealing his hand."

"What about the guy you saw running away, was it Harrison?" he asked.

I pressed my lips together. "I mean, it definitely fit his description. I didn't catch his face, though. We need to go ask him where he was today. Add some pressure."

"Bad cop, worse cop?" Dean asked.

I smiled. "Exactly."

"Okay, come and pick me up."

It was late. I'd spent an hour at the hospital already talking to the cops, hoping Kirk would wake up. He hadn't. The nurse said he was in a trauma induced coma that could last for hours or even days.

"We'll track him down and hit him first thing in the morning," I said. "Is Fern still there?"

Dean laughed through his nose. "Yeah, she's been a very good caregiver. I feel like an absolute invalid."

"You're welcome," Fern said, her voice muffled through the phone.

"I'll be back in ten," I said. "Don't go anywhere."

Dean laughed. "Wasn't planning on it, actually."

* * *

I drove back to the office and walked inside. The last couple days had been so eventful it was hard to remember when I'd last slept. Or eaten, for that matter.

Fern stood up as I entered the office.

"Convince her to leave, Noah," Dean said from his convalescence on the couch.

"What do you mean?" I asked with a raised brow. "Where are you going?"

Fern rolled her eyes. "I'm supposed to be on a flight to San Francisco, but I can *cancel* it. It doesn't matter when Dean is hurt."

He pinched his brows together and crossed his arms. "Yes it *does* matter. I'm completely capable of taking care of myself. This is a huge opportunity for you. You need to take it."

Fern bit her lip.

"I can look after him," I offered. I almost immediately regretted it, and yet I'd said it.

"Really?" she asked.

"See?" Dean said. "I'm in good hands. Get to the airport before you miss your flight."

"I guess." She looked between the two of us. "If you're sure?"

I shrugged. "I'm sure."

"Okay, then." She leaned down and kissed Dean on the cheek. "No more detecting while I'm gone. You're going to stay right here safe and sound."

He nodded. "Yes, ma'am."

"And *you*." She pointed her finger into my chest. "If you let my friend get hurt again we're going to have a problem."

I furrowed my brow. "I'm trying my best, but you know how he is. He's just so easy to harm."

She cocked her head to the side in acknowledgment. "Yeah, I know. *Still*."

"Hey!" Dean shouted from the couch. "I'm not a child or a fragile doll. I can make decisions on my own, *thank you very much*."

"Call me if anything happens," Fern said, ignoring Dean entirely.

"Will do."

She waved goodbye and left us alone in the office.

Dean sat up further on the couch, slumping his head against the armrest. "So how's Kirk doing?" he asked.

I shrugged. "I don't know. The doctors couldn't give me a straight answer. He might wake up by tomorrow, or not at all."

He sucked in a breath through his teeth. "Damn."

"I know."

He swung his legs out over the side of the couch and started to push himself into a standing position. "I guess you better drive me home, we have an early morning tomorrow."

"*Uh*, you're not going anywhere," I said, crossing my arms.

"What?" He raised an eyebrow.

I pushed his shoulder to make him sit back down. "You're staying here. Someone just tried to kill us. I'm not letting you stay at your apartment all by yourself."

He frowned. "Fern was just being dramatic, you don't *actually* have to take care of me, Noah."

"Well...I already promised, so it's too late. You're staying here tonight and that's final."

"Well—"

I gave him a look.

He rolled his eyes. "*Fine.* Do you have an extra pillow at least?" He pushed on the cushions. "This couch is kinda stiff."

I shook my head. "Don't be ridiculous, you're going to sleep upstairs in a real bed. You're injured. Sleeping on a couch could make your knee worse."

He laughed. "I'm not going to steal your bed from you, Noah. I'm more than happy to sleep on the couch."

"It's not stealing if I'm offering," I said firmly.

He waffled. "Well, but then where are *you* going to sleep?"

I shrugged. "On the couch. Wouldn't be the first time." Whenever Malcolm and I had fought somehow I'd found myself down in the office on that couch.

He crossed his arms and pouted. "I'm not happy with this."

"Too bad. Now up and at 'em. We need some food."

He shook his head. "I doubt anything is open this late."

"I wasn't going to order out."

He raised an eyebrow. "You cook?"

"Well enough." I helped him stand, and then we ventured up the stairs to my apartment. Captain greeted us upon entering with slobbery kisses and bounds of energy.

"Nice to see you too, boy." Dean smiled and ruffled Captain's face.

I set him down in a chair at the breakfast table and went about looking for something to eat. My cupboards were bare—what a shocker. I found a box of pasta and a can of diced tomatoes. That could make something edible, right?

As I set a pot of water on the stove to boil I tried to think of the last time I'd cooked for someone. Had it really been Malcolm? Over six months ago, maybe longer.

I set a glass of water on the table.

"Um, thanks." Dean was stiff, not his usual boisterous self.

"What's wrong?" I asked. "Are you in pain? Do you need to take something?"

He shook his head. "I'm just not used to being taken care of like this, that's all."

I laughed. "I wouldn't call this taking care of you. You haven't tried the pasta yet. It might kill you."

He grinned, his eyes bright. "I'm sure it'll be fine." He looked over at the stove. "What else do you have in the fridge?"

I shrugged. "I don't know." I looked inside to investigate.

"There," he pointed into the fridge, "put in some of that onion and that carrot."

I grabbed the items and smiled. "Yes, sir. Do you cook?"

He nodded. "All the time. You get good at cooking when you grow up poor."

I chuckled. "That's not always true, statistically. I've met a lot of poor people who wouldn't know a pot from a kettle."

He laughed through his nose. "Okay, well, I learned to cook from a young age. My mom was sick all the time—we didn't know why yet—and my dad was one of those pot and kettle people. My mom used to say that if he *could* burn water he *would*." He smiled. "Anyway, I learned to cook from the cooking channel. We didn't have cable, but my neighbor did. She was an older woman, and she sat around and watched TV all day long with her cats. She let me sit and watch with her."

I smiled. "That sounds nice."

He nodded. "It was. I learned how to make an omelette and started cooking my mom breakfast in the mornings when she couldn't get out of bed. Then I cooked anything I could get my hands on. Of course, whenever I messed up real bad my dad always made me eat it anyway." His face fell. "Said we couldn't waste food."

I held up the carrot and said, "What do I do with this?"

Dean laughed. "Chop it up real small. Do you own a knife?"

I glared at him. "Of course I own a knife."

He threw his hands up in defense. "Just asking."

We sat and talked while I cooked the pasta and our homemade sauce. The moment of truth came about half an hour later when I plated two servings of the pasta.

I was too scared to eat the first bite, so I waited for Dean's reaction. He grinned and laughed, almost spitting up his bite. "It's good, actually."

"*Really?*" I didn't believe him.

"Yes."

I took a bite of the pasta, and sure enough, it *was* pretty okay.

"Did your parents ever teach you how to make Korean food?" he asked.

I shook my head. "Nah, neither of my parents really cook. I ate a lot of my grandparents' cooking from their restaurant, but they died when I was young, and my dad sold the space to some other Korean family."

"Bummer."

I looked down at the table. "It is what it is."

We ate our pasta and talked about anything *but* the case. It was a nice change of pace, and I almost forgot that we'd been targeted today.

After we finished eating, it was late. Cooking the pasta had taken longer than I'd expected. "Um," Dean started. "I can't exactly sleep in this suit." He'd already taken off his suit jacket and rolled his sleeves up for a more relaxed look.

"Right." I should have thought of that. "You can borrow something of mine." It wouldn't be the first time, either. I grabbed an old sleep t-shirt—one of the non-embarrassing ones—and sleep shorts for him to wear. "Here." I handed him the stack.

"You don't have to sleep on the couch, you know," he said, a hint of a smile on his lips. "Your bed fits two."

I shook my head. "Dean, don't."

He widened his eyes with faux innocence. "*What?*"

"You know *what*," I said sternly.

He laughed and pushed my shoulder. "Okay, okay, you got me. Foiled again, detective."

A warmth ran through me and settled in my chest. The way he laughed. His smile. "Captain can keep you company," I offered. "Plus he's an okay guard dog."

He laughed through his nose. "Wow, really upselling him aren't you?"

209

I shrugged. "Sometimes he gets distracted. Hopefully tonight is a good night for him."

He chuckled. "Thanks. For everything, really."

I put my hands in my pockets and looked at the wall. "What else are bosses for?"

After an awkward pause, I left the room with my own pajamas under my arm and headed towards the door. "I'll be downstairs. If you need anything, just shout."

"Great plan," he said. "I can't exactly escape by myself, now can I?"

I nodded. "I'll make sure the doors are locked." I slipped out of the apartment and paused on the doorstep. Dean was *alone* in my bedroom. In my bed. I suddenly pictured every last item I didn't want him to snoop and find. "Damn." He'd better keep his hands to himself. The box of Malcolm's things in the closet, the ring on the bedside table, the messy pile of crap I'd shoved under the bed instead of dealing with it like an adult.

After double-checking that all the doors were locked I let myself back into the office and laid down on the couch. It was *much* harder than I remembered. I shifted, trying to get my back comfortable. Tonight was going to be a long night, and tomorrow was going to be an even longer day.

"Goodnight, Dean," I mumbled as I drifted off to sleep.

FIFTEEN

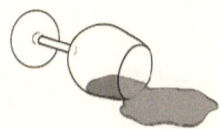

"Morning," a voice called, waking me from my sleep.

I checked my wrist immediately, forgetting I'd set my watch down on the coffee table last night. It was late in the morning, later than I'd intended.

Dean was standing in the doorway to the office carrying a carafe of coffee in one hand and two white mugs in the other. Captain was just behind him and nudged his way inside the room, finding me instantly.

"Morning?" I said, rubbing my bleary eyes.

"I made coffee, well, tried to make coffee," he said. "I wasn't sure how you usually make it, so I just winged it."

I pushed myself up into a sitting position and realized that Dean was still wearing my clothes from last night. They looked good on him.

The pajama shorts showed off his long muscular legs, and I realized that I'd never seen his legs before. Was that a strange thing to notice? His furry chest was peaking out from underneath the edge of the stretched out t-shirt.

"What are you doing?" I asked, pulling myself back to reality. "Why are you making me coffee? You should be sitting down, resting."

He blew out a breath and pinched his brows. "Nah, coffee trumps all else, right?" He placed the carafe of coffee and the two cups on the table.

I looked down at myself—I was still wearing my own pajamas. This was turning into a strange sort of slumber party that I wasn't accustomed to. Dean was barefoot, and he looked so casual in the space, relaxed. He sat down on the couch beside my stretched out legs and poured each of us a cup.

He handed me the mug, and I took a tentative sip. Not bad, a little weak, but not bad.

He seemed to read my mind. "I used the scoop by the tin of coffee grounds and just hoped that was the right amount. Is it good?"

I smiled despite myself. "Perfect."

He beamed. "Good. Now let's get to work. We still need to catch Harrison. But can we swing by the hospital first? I want to pay my respects to Kirk."

"Sure." I wanted an update on Kirk anyway. Hopefully if he woke up he could tell us who had attacked him.

We drank our coffees for a minute in comfortable silence. The hot liquid traveled down my throat and warmed my whole chest. Dean was resting back against my legs, and it didn't feel strange at all. It felt completely normal. That worried me. I meant what I'd said to Dean, that we shouldn't date. The kiss—while it had felt right in the moment—had been a mistake. Dean was working for me, or *with* me, and we needed to keep those lines drawn. I didn't need to end up in another Malcolm situation again. Dean was turning out to be a pretty good partner, and I didn't want to sacrifice his good instincts and growing skills for a single kiss. I couldn't afford to take that kind of risk.

"I don't suppose we can stop at my apartment too?" he asked. "Wearing the same suit three days in a row just feels icky." He shuddered.

Oh the horror. I laughed and took another sip of my coffee. "Okay, we can do that. I don't think Harrison is going anywhere anytime soon, at least, not until that will is found."

"Should we take Captain with us?" Dean asked.

Hearing his name, Captain nuzzled his face in-between the cushions and our frames.

"*Hmm*, maybe." I raised a brow. "Do you think he's intimidating enough to scare Harrison?"

Dean grinned. "Oh, definitely. Look at that face."

I looked down at Captain and wasn't convinced. Captain was too cute, too fluffy. Especially with his tongue hanging out and his tail wagging with content like that. He'd made for a terrible guard dog, but an amazing companion since Malcolm left.

He slapped my bare knee, shocking me. "Okay, let's go."

"Ow." I rubbed my leg. "Personal space, Dean."

He only smirked.

We got up and got dressed. Then I drove Dean to his apartment to change. He chose a pale, pewter blue suit fitting for the LA weather and paired it with a cherry red tie. It was almost theatrical in nature. "You look ridiculous," I said as Dean straightened the tie.

He nodded. "Thank you."

I laughed through my nose and followed him back out to the car.

When we reached the hospital, there was a police officer standing outside Kirk's room. Good, at least they were doing something right. Luckily, the guy knew who I was and after showing him my detective license he let us inside. A nurse was standing over the hospital bed writing something down on a clipboard.

"Any change?" I asked.

She looked up and shook her head. "No, nothing yet." She pointed to a monitor over to the side. "We're tracking his brain waves, and we should be able to see when his activity improves. Or of course, you know, he'll wake up."

I nodded. "Thanks."

The nurse left and we were alone in the room. The heart monitor beeped steadily, and there was a sterile alcohol smell in the air.

"Sorry you got screwed over," Dean said quietly to Kirk. He'd put his knee brace back on and seemed to be walking a little bit better which gave me hope that the twist wasn't as bad as I'd first thought.

"Not to speak ill of the wounded," I said, "but the man *did* barricade himself inside with a killer."

Dean narrowed his eyes at me. "*Unknowingly.*"

I shrugged. "Yes, unknowingly."

We stayed like that for a few minutes, watching Kirk breathe in and out. He didn't have a tube in his throat, which looked like a good sign to me, however I was no doctor. He might never wake up. That would make him the third innocent victim in this case.

"If only you could tell us what we need to know," Dean said, half to himself, half to Kirk.

"If only," I repeated. Unfortunately, telepathy was a myth.

After a few seconds Dean asked, "Did he have anything on him?"

"Like what?"

He shrugged. "I don't know. I'm just thinking about Heather's unsent text. Maybe we'll get lucky and Kirk did something similar."

"I doubt it." I looked around the room and spotted a blue plastic bag sitting on the table—the kind hospitals usually use to store the patient's personal effects. "There." I pointed at the bag, and Dean pulled it onto the bed between us.

He sifted through the contents and sighed. "It's just his clothes. Nothing useful."

As I thought it would be.

"Wait." A flash of blue caught my eye. I'd almost missed it since the bag was also blue. Tucked into the back pocket of Kirk's jeans was a folded up piece of paper.

"What is that?" Dean asked, hunching over the bed to see.

I unfolded the paper, and I was right. "It's another blackmail note." It was written on the same pale blue letterhead from the theater, just like all the others.

"What's it say?" Dean asked.

I cleared my throat and read aloud, "Five thousand or your man gets exposed and you along with him. No more hiding in the shadows. Your boyfriend will finally be caught in the bright, hot lights."

"Kinda wordy," Dean said quietly, before catching himself. "I mean, it's not like the other notes, is it?"

"No," I agreed. It was totally different from the short and sweet blackmail notes Heather had shown us. "Maybe Kirk wrote this after he had his big fight with Caroline?" I guessed. "He was angry, pissed off. The note got personal. It could be that he was thinking of sending it, only he never did. Look at the paper." The page was worn, and the letters were faded.

"It looks like it's been through the wash," he said.

I nodded. "Exactly. I think Kirk realized it was a mistake to send this note, and so he didn't end up going through with it. He must have forgotten about it in the pocket of these jeans."

"Wow, so how does this help us?" he asked. "What does he mean? Hiding in the shadows? The lights?" Dean's eyes went wide. "Harrison is the lighting director! He's always in the shadows because he's *behind* the lights, not on stage with the actors." Dean reached out and gripped my arm tight. "This is basically Kirk *confirming* that the boyfriend is Harrison!"

"I think you might be right." I racked my brain on how the cryptic poem could be interpreted differently, and Harrison was the most obvious answer. The bright, hot lights? It *had* to be Harrison.

"This is amazing. Another piece of the puzzle." Dean grinned, realized he was still gripping my arm, and let go. "Sorry."

"That's okay." I didn't even care. It was only Dean.

"What are you two doing here?" a low voice snapped.

I turned toward the door, past the gauzy hospital curtains. Robert was standing in the open doorway holding a small bouquet of flowers.

"What?" I looked at Dean in confusion and then back to Robert.

"Haven't you two done enough already?" he asked, a hard edge to his voice. His pale eyes were narrowed, and his brow was furrowed.

"Um, we were just paying our respects," I said, not understanding his tone or demeanor. Why was he angry?

"By riffling through his things?" Robert asked, pointing down at the blue plastic bag on the bed.

"Uh..." Dean was socially stumped, same as me, having been called out.

"Leave, now!" he barked.

"Mr. Hydecker—" I started, trying to diffuse the situation.

"I thought I made it clear when I told you your services were no longer acquired, but apparently you can't follow simple instructions." He turned toward the police officer guarding the door. "These two are not supposed to be here, escort them out. Now!"

Was he being serious? What the hell was happening?

I slipped the faded blackmail note into my back pocket as subtly as I could, hoping nobody would notice.

The officer gave us a perplexed look, but since Robert was the one with the money and was, no doubt, footing the bill on Kirk's room, he did as he was asked. "Sorry guys," he whispered as he led us out of the room.

"Just because you ended our agreement doesn't make the case closed," I shouted back at Robert, letting my emotions slip out. He wasn't paying us anymore, so what right did he have to demand that we leave?

He snarled. "I don't know what you're trying to stir up by continuing to *harass* my employees, but this case certainly *is* closed. If I find you two snooping around, or asking any more questions, I'll have Detective Warner arrest you," he threatened. "And I know that you harassed Camilla as well, even though I told you not to talk to her. I didn't peg you two as incompetent, but clearly I was wrong."

Gone was the teary-eyed widower that we'd witnessed a couple days ago. Robert was all hard edges and venom today. What had changed between then and now?

Dean tugged on my arm and pulled me from my trance down the hall.

"Um, so apparently I was right and Robert is definitely guilty of something, yeah?" Dean asked once we were at the end of the hall waiting in front of the elevators.

"Uh, yeah." I was totally bamboozled. How had Robert turned on us so quickly? And why? I'd thought that maybe his judgment had been clouded by grief, but now I was questioning that idea too.

We rode the elevator down to the parking garage and got in the Jeep.

"I mean, I told you from the start he was suspicious," Dean said. "Now he's acting like this? He can't seriously deny that this is all connected, can he? There's been two murders and two attempted murders already, and it's only been a few days."

"I know." I secretly wished that I'd listened to Dean earlier, but I'd been too stubborn. I'd wanted to be right so badly I'd ignored the most obvious suspect we had. It's always the spouse. "I'm starting to agree with you. Robert is overcompensating for something. There's no way that was all caused by grief. We're getting close to finding the killer, and he doesn't want us to."

"What does that mean for the investigation?" Dean asked. "That Robert is working *with* the killer? That they're partners? I thought maybe he'd just hired someone. You know, a freelancer."

I tapped my hand against the steering wheel. "But it would make sense, right? I mean, think about it—how could one person be zipping across town doing all these things? How could someone be trying to run us over while at the same time searching through the theater for the will?"

"*Hmm*, yeah, you're right," he said. There's just that one problem: Robert's alibi."

I shook my head. "That's no problem."

He raised a brow. "It's not?"

"It's the same as if Robert *had* hired someone. He was holed up in Newport Beach with Camilla while Harrison was out killing Caroline."

"But *why* would they be working together?" he asked. "Just for the money?"

I scoffed. "Does there need to be another motive? Isn't greed enough?"

"I guess so." It was silent in the car. Even the parking garage was surprisingly quiet. "So what now?" he asked.

I tightened my grip on the steering wheel, my knuckles turning white. "Now we catch the bastard."

Dean grinned. "Sounds good to me."

SIXTEEN

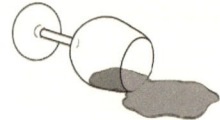

"So are we going to confront Harrison?" Dean asked.

I shook my head and started the engine. "Change of plans. Now that we're assuming it's the two of them working together we need to gather evidence on Robert as well. Otherwise the cops will just arrest Harrison and Robert will get off scot-free. We can't let that happen."

He hummed. "So what did you have in mind?"

I twisted my hands along the steering wheel. "Several things, but first we need to find that car. Robert must have been the one who tried to run us over. Think about it. We go to the theater to confront Tim, and magically when we get to Runway magazine someone is there trying to run us over? Harrison was probably at the theater and tipped Robert off that we were still investigating even after he'd fired us. So he zipped over to the magazine and waited for us to walk out into the garage."

"That makes sense. But how do we find the car?" Dean asked. "We don't even know the make and model."

I let out a long sigh. "Now comes the hard part." I pulled out my phone and looked up a list of auto body shops across LA. There were hundreds of them. Dean and I started calling, asking if anyone had brought in a black sedan with damage to the front fender. We were well over an hour in, and had called about two dozen shops, when we realized we weren't getting anywhere. Trying to strong-arm the case wasn't going to work. We needed to be smarter than that.

"Maybe he didn't try to get the car fixed?" Dean said after hanging up on his tenth call.

I cocked my head to the side. "I guess that's possible. I just really hoped he would try to fix it. That would have made this so much easier. Although, I guess at his income bracket maybe he simply dumped the car instead. We could just replace it with another."

Dean groaned. "If he dumped it we'll never find it."

"*Hmm*, not necessarily. You'd be surprised. You can't exactly drive a car off a cliff and have it go unnoticed these days."

"But how would *we* find it?" he asked. "We're not the cops. We don't have access to tip lines, or witness statements, or anything like that.

I racked my brain. Where would Robert dump a car? It had to be close by since we'd seen him in the city every day of the investigation. He couldn't have driven too far away, or we would have noticed. Then there was the trouble of getting back to the city without a car. There was no way he'd towed it somewhere, right? That would have been too obvious, too flagrant.

"Wait." Something had been nagging at the back of my mind since yesterday, and it finally clicked together. I'd discounted Robert, which had been a mistake. Now that I had my head on straight and was looking at things clearly, I saw what I'd been missing. It was so obvious, I was mentally kicking myself.

"What?" Dean asked.

I grinned. "I think I know where the car is."

"Really?" He raised a brow. "Where?"

"I'll show you."

* * *

I drove across Hollywood back to the magazine's office building downtown. Back to the scene of the almost hit-and-run.

"Why are we here?" Dean asked with pinched brows.

"Because," I started, before cutting the engine, "I realized something about yesterday that I'd forgotten. Something important."

"Which was what?"

"What do you see?" I asked, pointing to the packed underground garage.

He searched the parking lot, craning his neck to look in all directions. "Uh, a bunch of cars? What am I supposed to be seeing?"

I didn't blame him for missing it, I'd missed it too, and it had been so obvious. Right in front of our faces, like he was taunting us.

"Come on." I got out of the car, and Dean followed behind me. The smell of gas and sunbaked asphalt filled the air. Across the lot, the back corner was shrouded in shadow. That's why I hadn't noticed it right away.

"What are we looking for?" Dean asked right before he noticed. A fleet of three, identical black sedans were parked next to each other in a row. Their dark exteriors blended seamlessly into the shadows, and there were no lights above them unlike the rest of the garage.

Dean pointed at the line of cars. "Oh my God, is that the same car?"

My hunch had been correct.

"Well it's obvious which one he borrowed, isn't it?" I said. The rest of the fleet was pristine and well polished, except for the standout in the middle, which had scratches and black marks along the front bumper from where Robert had crashed into the ticket gate.

"He brought the car back?" Dean said, in shock. "Without fixing it? He just drove it back?"

I shook my head. "I don't know what he was thinking. He probably panicked. He didn't have time to fix it before he needed to return it. Someone at the company would have noticed sooner or later. This must have been Caroline's personal fleet of company cars that drove her to and from work every day. That's how Robert knew they were here. It was the perfect vehicle, since it was already waiting for him. When Harrison tipped him off that we were visiting the office that day, Robert didn't have much time to pull a plan together."

Dean scoffed. "What was he going to do if he *had* killed us? Just wipe the blood off the bumper and put it back?"

I crossed my arms. "I don't know. Maybe he would have dumped it, or maybe he was going to blame the whole thing on Harrison and throw him under the bus. Who knows?"

I was shocked at his stupidity, but based on his swift personality change earlier at the hospital, he must have been feeling backed into a corner, willing to break character as the nice, grieving widower.

I took pictures of the cars and the damage with my phone for evidence. Warner was going to have a fun time explaining this away.

Dean frowned. "Wait. How'd you know these were here?"

I gestured with my hand. "I just suddenly remembered that as we got out of the elevator there were these bright headlights shining from that back corner. I'd totally forgotten about it when we didn't know who was trying to kill us, but when I added Robert to the equation it all started to make sense."

"That wasn't very smart of him, was it?"

"No, it wasn't." I shook my head. "He didn't have much time. Maybe he made a split-second decision? Or he thought it was better than trying to kill us with his own car? Either way, he didn't plan on us surviving the attempt, so maybe it didn't matter to him that the car was easily recognizable."

"I wonder if this parking garage has security footage?" Dean asked, looking up at the cement beams.

I nodded. "I was wondering the same thing. If so, the police can use that as further proof of attempted murder."

"Is that enough?" he asked, crossing his arms. "To catch him?"

I shook my head. "The video won't prove that Robert was the one driving, unless his face is caught on camera, but I somehow doubt he would let that happen. He must have known there were cameras down here since he was familiar with the garage."

Dean frowned. "So we need something else?" He sighed. "What else is left?"

"We need a trap." I grinned. "And I think I know *just* the one."

* * *

We went back to the office and started plotting, writing down everything we knew about Robert, Harrison, and their connection to one another. There wasn't much.

"They both work at the theater, and they both love their jobs," Dean listed off. "They both had a motive to kill Caroline—Robert would inherit the theater and Harrison would get her money if she added him to her will like we think she did. They both fought with her." He pressed his lips together. "I don't know, it's a lot, but also at the same time, not a lot. Nothing concrete."

I was about to reply when my phone began to ring. I thought maybe it was my mom and was going to silence the call, but the number was from the police department. "Hello?" I answered.

"Mr. Sun, it's Detective Warner here. I just received a call from a very angry Mr. Hydecker who says that you are now harassing him?"

I pulled the phone away from my mouth and sighed. *What the hell?* I didn't have time for this crap.

"Hello?" Warner said again, more agitated this time.

"Yes, hi," I replied. "I was not harassing Mr. Hydecker. If anything, Mr. Hydecker was harassing *me*."

"I highly doubt that, Mr. Sun. You have one warning. If I hear that you've spoken to Mr. Hydecker or his employees again, I'll have to arrest you for obstruction and harassment. And I don't want to have to do that."

Sure you do. "Okay, I hear you loud and clear." *Idiot.*

"Good. Glad you can see reason, Mr. Sun. I'll let Mr. Hydecker know that he won't be seeing any more of you."

"Okay, *bye, bye, now.*" I hung up the phone and narrowly avoided throwing it across the room.

Dean raised an eyebrow. "What the hell was that?"

"Apparently Robert is feeling the pressure. He told Warner we were harassing him, and Warner said if we didn't stop he'd arrest us."

Dean blew out a quick breath. "What a ninny."

I sighed. "Exactly. Now, where were we?"

"Catching the bastard," he reminded me.

I snapped my fingers. "Exactly."

Dean continued where he left off with his list. We still didn't have much connecting the two men.

Lexi showed up not long after. I'd texted her with an update on the case, and she'd insisted on helping. I was glad for the extra brain power. "I brought snacks," she announced, carrying a bag of goodies.

"Amazing, one can't solve a murder on an empty stomach," Dean said with a lopsided grin.

Lexi rolled her eyes and sat down between us on the couch. "So, the husband was in on it after all? I thought he had an alibi?"

"Looks like it. He was playing us the whole time," I said—not feeling bitter at all. "Now that we're on to him, he got nasty and revealed his hand. He called Warner and said we were harassing him. We just need to trap him in a lie. Get him to confess."

"So what?" She pursed her lips in thought. "You're going to confront him and record the conversation?"

I shook my head. "Too risky. I've done it before, and I left with a black eye. Not repeating that mistake."

She sucked in a sharp breath through her teeth. "Oh, I remember that. Yeah, that was early days, huh? Malcolm was *not* happy."

"When was he ever?" I mumbled under my breath.

Dean bit into a corner store beef stick. "So what's the plan, boss?"

I laced my fingers together and leaned back in the chair. "I'm thinking Hardy Boys. The misdirect."

Lexi grinned, reading my mind as always. "Perfect."

SEVENTEEN

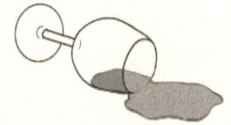

It was easy to forge the two notes since we already had handwriting samples from both our suspects—from when Harrison had written his friend's name down on my notepad and a note Robert had left in Tim's office. Lexi was a mastermind with a pen.

"How are you so good at that?" Dean asked in awe as Lexi finished the last note.

She shrugged. "I don't know. My parents sent me to a calligraphy camp when I was a kid, maybe that's why. It's just kinda easy for me."

"Man, if I was still conning I could use your skills," Dean said.

I frowned. "But you're *not* still conning, and neither is my teenage niece."

He grinned. "I was just joking, Noah. *Relax.*"

"Right."

We used the same blue letterhead from the theater that Dean had pocketed earlier and sent out the letters immediately by messenger so they would arrive that same afternoon.

"I hope this works," Dean said.

It was a risk, for sure. No doubt, they usually communicated by text or in person. We had no way of knowing if they ever sent notes to each other. I was hoping that even if it seemed out of character they'd be comfortable enough to follow directions.

"It will." I handed him a walkie-talkie. "Now, you're going to stay in constant contact with me, right?"

He nodded. "Of course."

"Good, let's go over the plan one more time." I said, my palms sweaty.

Dean rolled his eyes, but did as I asked. "I'll be following Harrison, you'll be following Robert. When they meet up, we're going to film their interaction, and hopefully whatever they say will be enough to get them both convicted, or at least force the police to do their jobs and actually arrest them."

"Yes, and you're going to..."

He grinned and shook my shoulders. "*Keep in contact with you at all times.* You've repeated yourself twice, Noah. I'm not an invalid."

I nodded. "Good."

He raised an eyebrow. "Good that I'm not an invalid, or good that I remember the plan?"

I frowned. "*Both*, I hope."

He grinned. "Right. See you on the other side."

With Fern in San Francisco, Lexi was our only backup. She was on her computer in the office, tracking both of our phones. She could call the cops in case anything happened. "You guys are just going to film them, right?" she confirmed. "Don't interact with either of them. Especially now that Robert is spooked. He's on the defensive. He's already tried to kill you once, he won't hesitate to try again."

"Yes, I know, Niece." I nodded. "Thank you for the advice."

She frowned and placed a hand on her hip. "You don't have to be belittling."

I pinched my brows and kissed her on the cheek. "What'd I say?"

She rolled her eyes. "Whatever, just be safe." She pointed at Dean. "That goes for you too. Don't do anything stupid."

He placed his hand on his chest and pulled his brows together. "Me? Unsafe? Whatever are you implying?"

"We'll be safe," I said for the both of us, pushing Dean toward the door.

"You better!" she called as we left the office.

Since Fern was out of town, and Dean's Speedster was a pile of rubble in a junkyard somewhere, he was driving her car while I was driving the

Jeep. We'd delivered the notes very discreetly half an hour ago to give us some lead time. We'd instructed in the notes to meet up at three o'clock. It was almost two. So we had some time, but we needed to catch our suspects before they left.

I was about to hop in the Jeep when Dean tugged on my shoulder. "What?" I asked as he pulled me into a hug. "*Oh*, okay." Were we hugging now? I wanted to move away, but the warmth and pressure of him relaxed my nerves. I wasn't usually nervous before stakeouts or before I shadowed someone. Today was more important. We owed it to Caroline and Heather to catch the bastards.

"Be safe," Dean whispered near my ear before letting me go.

My neck was flushed, and I avoided his eyes. "I'm always safe. You know me well enough by now."

"*Hmm*, that's what I'm worried about," he said.

I scoffed. "Why don't you focus on keeping *you* safe? I can take care of myself."

He gave me a look like he didn't believe me before backing away. "Okay, if you say so."

Why was he suddenly so concerned with my safety? Then again, why was I so concerned with his? I chalked it up to employer ethics. To being a responsible adult. But deep down I knew it was more than that. I liked Dean, and I didn't want to see him get hurt.

234

I got in the Jeep and, based on Lexi's information, drove toward Robert's neighborhood. We'd kept the notes vague on purpose so that they would come to their own conclusion about where to meet up. Wherever their *normal* spot was. If they had one. This plan could easily blow up in our faces, or simply, not work.

Once up in the hills, I parked under the shade of a large oak tree down the road from Robert's house. Shadowing 101: never get too close to your suspect. This was the only way out of the neighborhood—I'd see if he drove by.

The facts of the case played through my mind as I waited, my eyes trained on my rearview mirror. Caroline had let her killer inside the house. She'd moved the dog upstairs. Harrison had gotten her drunk, which didn't seem like a hard task according to Heather, and then somehow forced her to take the pills. She must have been *very* drunk. Did he use a pipe? Or did he just shove them down her throat? Then he would have had to wait for the pills to work, or else they wouldn't show up in her blood toxicology. So once Caroline was passed out, on the verge of death, Harrison had carried her out to the pool and pushed her in. Making it look like either an accident or a suicide.

How long would the whole event have taken? An hour? Less? The footage from the bird lady showed Harrison leaving around ten thirty, however he never came back. So where did he go after he killed her? To Robert? No, that would have been stupid, and besides we were watching

Robert that night when he was with Camilla. We didn't stay all night, just long enough to get our photos, but there was no way that they had met up on Friday. So where did Harrison go? Why did he leave behind so much sloppy evidence? Heather noticed the inconsistencies right away. Did everything go to plan, or were there hiccups that changed his course?

My thoughts were drowned out when I spotted Robert's silver BMW coming around the bend. He'd taken the bait. I waited for him to get about a hundred feet ahead of me before I started the engine and followed behind him. "Robert is on the move," I said into the walkie-talkie. "Status update?"

Dean's voice came in, mechanical and fuzzy, "Harrison hasn't left yet. He's still at this record shop downtown. Do you think they're meeting there?"

"We'll find out."

I followed Robert south from the hills toward Hollywood. Was it possible they were meeting at a record shop? Out in the open? How would they ever explain that away? That's not what I was expecting. I guess I'd thought they would meet in some seedy back alley somewhere away from prying eyes. I don't know. Something more secretive.

After a few minutes sitting in standstill LA traffic Dean said something else, "He's leaving now."

So no record shop. "Okay, just keep your distance, remember?"

"Got it."

236

The light turned green and we finally started moving. Robert turned right, in the direction of West Hollywood. Toward the theater.

"It looks like he's heading to the theater," I said over the walkie-talkie.

"Um, Harrison is going south," Dean said.

Strange. Was this a misdirect, or was Robert doing something else? "Maybe Robert is grabbing something from the theater before meeting Harrison. He still has time." I looked at my watch. It was only 2:45. Though fifteen minutes didn't mean much in LA. "Just stay on him," I said.

"*Roger that, over.*"

I rolled my eyes.

Two turns later and Robert was pulling into the back lot of the theater just as I'd predicted. *Should I follow him inside?* What was he grabbing that he needed in order to meet Harrison? Was it evidence? Was he *getting rid* of evidence? Was there rehearsal today? Had he even read the note?

Questions filled my brain as I tried to make a decision on what to do. "He stopped at the theater," I said into the walkie-talkie. "I'm going in. Stay on Harrison. I'm going radio silent. I'll text you if I need you."

Dean's mechanical voice buzzed back, "Okay, don't do anything stupid."

I grinned. "Right back at you."

I parked across the street on the busy boulevard and jogged to the back of the theater. I caught Robert just as he was slipping inside the door. Did they ever lock that damn door? It seemed like a huge security issue.

I gave him a few seconds of lead time before testing the handle, slowly pulling it open, and creeping inside. It was dark, almost pitch black in the hallway. The lights were off. Surely the theater would start to come alive soon for an evening rehearsal. Was anyone else here? The parking lot had looked deserted.

I heard the groaning of the floorboards and the clicking of Robert's dress shoes ahead of me in the dark. He probably knew the layout of the theater better than his own home. Robert had gone past the spiral stairs toward the stage. So he wasn't going to his office. What was he grabbing on stage?

I walked forward into the dark until I reached the doorway. I cracked the door open just enough to listen in.

Robert's heavy voice filled the quiet theater. "Are you here?"

Shit, was someone else meeting him? Was Harrison supposed to be here right now? Had there been a mix up? Why was Harrison driving south while Robert was already at the theater?

I scrambled up the spiral stairs, remembering the great view of the stage from the catwalk. *I should be able to see him from up there.* The old metal stairs *squeaked*, and I cursed. If Robert heard me, he didn't react.

Maybe I was far enough away, or the stage was so echoey that the noise hadn't even reached him. I climbed the rest of the stairs as carefully as possible until I reached the open air catwalk above the stage. I hid behind a wooden crate and peered down at Robert.

The stage was dark, but only for a moment. Bright spotlights suddenly filled the center of the floor. Robert was standing with his hands on his hips, alone. Then another figure walked onto the stage from the side. "I'm here. What was so urgent that it couldn't wait until tonight?" a voice called. A tenor, male voice. Not Harrison's deep, gravelly tone.

I clamped a hand across my mouth as Jake Amarov walked into the spotlight.

EIGHTEEN

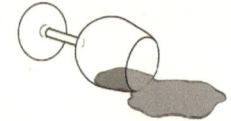

Jake? Why was Jake here? Where was Harrison?

And suddenly it all fell into place. It was Jake, *not* Harrison that was working with Robert. We'd discounted Jake from being Caroline's boyfriend because we'd thought he was gay. Well, he was an actor after all. I was sure he could act his way into inheriting tens of millions of dollars.

In the dark, Jake and Harrison looked fairly similar. Gigi must have seen Jake with his toned body and dark hair. From the back it would be hard to tell.

"What do you mean?" Robert hissed. "You sent *me* that note."

"What?" Jake narrowed his eyes and took a step back. "What is this?" He looked left and right across the stage. "I didn't send you a note."

Robert took a second before he said, "You didn't?"

Jake shook his head.

"I didn't send *you* a note either," Robert said softly, his rage calming.

Jake put his hands on his hips and said, "Someone set us up."

Shit. I pulled out my phone to text Dean that Harrison was the wrong guy, and also to *not* follow me to the theater. Only, I had no bars. Dammit. The heavy cement walls of the theater must have been a dead zone for service. I hadn't thought of that. I still had the walkie-talkie, but if I made *any* noise they'd find me immediately. I had no way of telling Dean to be quiet either. He could easily give me away if he opened his big mouth.

"It was probably those goddamn detectives that Heather hired," Robert said, looking around the theater for someone listening in on them. "Were you followed?" he asked.

Jake shook his head. "No way. I would have noticed."

Robert frowned, his hands on his hips. "Or not, that's the whole point of being followed."

"Were *you*?" Jake asked accusingly, taking a step back.

"No, definitely not," Robert said sternly. "I told you those two would be trouble."

"That's why you were supposed to get rid of them, Robert," Jake stage whispered. "I held up my side of the bargain and got Caroline out of the picture."

Shit, I should be recording this. I pulled out my phone and started recording video, angling the phone around the corner of the crate. It was probably terrible footage. Hopefully my witness testimony would be enough by itself.

"Well, how the hell was I supposed to know that Caroline was going to hire those goons to follow me and Camilla?" Robert asked, waving his arms wildly.

"You said you were on top of it," Jake snapped.

Robert's voice softened. "Baby, I am."

Baby? What the hell?

I peered around the crate, past the metal railing, at the pair. Robert had his hands on Jake's shoulders, and in a flash he pulled him in for an embrace. "Don't worry about anything."

"Don't worry?" Jake said, his pitch rising. "We still haven't found that stupid will. I don't want to be blindsided if Caroline lied to me about adding me to her inheritance. What if she lied?"

Robert ran a hand through Jake's tousled dark hair. "She didn't. She would have done anything to get that money away from me. It was the perfect plan, baby. Relax. We're almost at the end."

"Well what about those notes?" he whined. "What are we supposed to do now?"

Robert looked around the theater once more. "Clearly something went wrong because we're the only ones here. Maybe it was a bluff? I mean, no one suspects a thing. If the cops had evidence against us we'd be in handcuffs already."

A *creak* echoed across the theater. Both Robert and Jake spun in the direction of the noise.

"We're not alone," Jake whispered.

It wasn't me. I hadn't moved a muscle. Was someone else from the theater here? To set up for rehearsals?

Robert pointed stage left. "You stand back there, and I'll wait for our guest. I bet it's those damn detectives. I'd say it's time we end their investigation once and for all, wouldn't you?"

Jake grinned. "Agreed." They kissed and separated across the stage.

No, it couldn't be Dean they heard. I'd told Dean to stay on Harrison. There was no way he would follow me into the theater, especially after I'd told him specifically not to. Right?

"Hello?" Dean's voice called.

My heart dropped into my stomach.

"Robert?" Dean said, his loud voice echoing across the theater. "I just wanted to apologize about yesterday."

What is he doing? I couldn't move an inch or they'd know where I was. I couldn't help him, couldn't warn him.

Dean walked out onto the stage, toward Robert. "Oh, there you are. I thought you might be here."

Robert smiled an unnervingly calm smile. "Dean. You were a good friend to my wife for years. I never told you how much I appreciated that. Caroline had so few friends."

What was their plan? Where had Jake gone? I couldn't see him past the side of the stage. I had to do something. This was an ambush. I stood up from my crouch and searched the catwalk. What could I do? How could I distract them? I spotted a heavy sandbag by the side of the doorway. I had no idea what the sandbag was for, but I knew how I was going to use it. This would have to be fast. Dean's life depended on it.

I surged forward, picked up the heavy sandbag, and tossed it over the catwalk toward the stage, aiming for an empty area away from the furniture and set walls. I didn't want to hit them, I just wanted to surprise them.

I didn't watch the outcome as I only had seconds to jump down the spiral stairs and book it toward the stage. When I got there, Dean was holding his fists up in a fighting stance, a mere step away from Robert who was too close for comfort. Jake was nowhere to be seen, which was worrying me. Where was he? I looked around, searching the empty stage. He must have been hiding behind one of the many layers of curtains. "There's two of them!" I shouted, taking my place beside Dean.

"Yeah, I got that," Dean said, his eyes concentrated on Robert.

I took a step forward. "Let's just calm down and talk." If I could just get him to stand still for a minute I could locate Jake.

"Okay, sure," Robert lowered his arms in compliance, but then his eyes darted behind me.

I didn't have time to turn before someone jumped me from behind, kicking my knees. I cried out and fell to the floor. Dean threw a wide punch at Robert which landed squarely on his chin. Robert let out a curse.

I scrambled on the ground to turn and face my attacker. Jake was grinning as he shoved me down and straddled my middle. "No luck, detective." All I remembered was a fist rapidly approaching my face. Then blackness.

NINETEEN

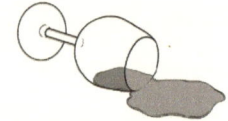

When I woke up, the first thing I noticed was that my arms were occupied, and my wrists hurt. "Shit." Blood pounded behind my eyes—I had a killer headache.

"You're finally awake," Dean said calmly.

We were still on stage, though the curtains were drawn behind us, hiding us from the auditorium. A few pieces of Edwardian furniture littered the space along with rugs and a lamp. It was set up like a living room in an old house, and momentarily made me question where I was.

I was sitting down in a chair, my arms tied behind my back to the frame with some kind of rope. I glanced over my shoulder. Dean was stuck in the same situation, his seat butting up against mine.

"Are you okay?" he asked.

I shrugged. "I've been better. Where are the two knuckleheads?"

"I don't know," he said. "I heard Jake say something about the inheritance. I think they're still looking for that will."

I shook my head. "Well it doesn't look like they're going to have much luck considering they've already ransacked two of the departments. Why would Caroline hide it here? She hated the theater."

"Maybe she thought she was being clever?" Dean offered. "Maybe she'd been having doubts about Jake."

It was warm up on stage with the lights beating down on our shoulders. My forehead was starting to glisten with sweat.

"I told you to stay on Harrison," I reminded him gently, though it didn't help much now.

"Harrison wasn't our guy!" Dean insisted. "He went from a record shop, to a thrift store, to a movie theater. He was having the time of his life. I was able to put two and two together that we'd been led astray. And you were all alone here at the theater without any backup!"

"Yeah, it was Jake," I said lamely.

"I know," he said. "It all fell together as soon as I realized Harrison wasn't the right guy. Kirk's message about the lights on stage? It wasn't about Harrison, it was about Jake, the lead actor who *was* on stage under the bright, hot lights."

I *almost* laughed. "Yeah, turns out we were trying too hard. The clue was simpler than that. Kirk was being literal. We thought that Jake couldn't be Caroline's boyfriend because he was gay, but—"

"People contain multitudes?" Dean offered.

I let out a long breath. "Sure."

"So how are we going to get out of this?" Dean asked.

I shook my head. "I don't know yet." I'd been thinking as we'd been talking, but nothing had come to mind.

"Well they're not going to leave us tied up forever. They're just waiting to kill us until *after* they find that will. Which might be soon," Dean reminded me.

"*I understand that, Dean.*" It was more than just the lights that were making me sweat. I'd been caught in a bind before during a case, but never quite so literally.

"*Ugh*, I saw them kissing," Dean said. "It was disgusting."

I nodded. "Me too."

"I can't believe I didn't see it coming."

I wriggled my wrists, but that only seemed to make the ropes feel tighter, the rough texture biting into my skin.

"I tried that already," Dean said, who must have heard the rustling of the cords. "Apparently Robert was a Boy Scout. I could have fought them off, only Jake had a knife on you and said I'd better sit myself down in this chair or he'd cut up your pretty face."

"He said I had a pretty face?" I asked, momentarily distracted.

Dean hummed. "Yeah, he also mumbled something in Russian that I couldn't quite understand. Something about your butt and slaying a dragon, I don't know."

"You speak Russian?" I asked, surprised.

"*Eh*, I speak a little of everything. Russian's not one of the strong ones," he said casually, like it was a normal everyday skill.

The things I learned about him constantly astounded me.

How *were* we going to get out of this? I tugged on the ropes again even though it hadn't worked the first time and got the same result. "At least you got one good punch in," I said. "I didn't know you could fight like that."

"Oh yeah," Dean said. "My grandpa taught me to box when I was a kid. Said I needed to learn to fight my bullies."

"Charming." Fighting in school would have gotten me grounded for life.

"So he was a little bit off the mark, but he meant well. It came in handy, didn't it?"

"Until I got us caught," I said.

"It's not your fault he ambushed you," Dean argued. "He played dirty."

I stretched out my legs to see how far I could reach, but there was no use. What was I going to do with my legs? Untie the ropes? Maybe I could break the chair like I'd seen done in movies. Only these chairs were thick, and metal—not some flimsy prop chair.

"Any solutions yet?" Dean asked, hopeful.

"*Hmm*, talk them into giving up?" I offered, truly out of options. "Maybe Lexi will notice we've been here for a long time and call the cops? I'm sure she's been texting me."

Dean let out a heavy breath. "Okay, so we just need to stall them from murdering us?"

I shrugged. "Essentially."

"Easy," Dean said. "I'm good at talking."

"We're *not* going to die," I assured him. I wasn't going to let anyone murder me *or* my partner. It was out of the question.

"But we *could*," he countered.

"Let's not go there. We *could* have died in a car crash on our way over here," I replied. "We're not dying today."

"Do you promise?" Dean asked.

I nodded, though he couldn't see me. "I promise."

"So...if we make it out of here alive—"

"Which we will," I interrupted.

He started over, "*When* we make it out of here alive...how about a date?"

I scoffed, which quickly turned into a laugh. "How can you be thinking about romance at a time like this? When we're waiting for two psychos to decide whether they want to murder us or not?"

"I'm always thinking about romance when I'm this close to you, Noah," Dean said with a soft, deep tone.

I was completely taken aback. "And now you're flirting?"

"I can't help myself!" Dean cried. "I'm nervous we're about to die. Can't you go along with the fantasy? Distract me?"

I let out a deep breath, a rush of blood heading up my neck and ears. "Okay. If we make it out of here alive...I'll go on a date with you. *Just one*. And it doesn't mean anything," I insisted.

"*When*," he said.

"What?" I shook my head. "I don't know, any time."

"No, you said *if* we get out of here," he clarified. "But you promised me *when*."

"Yes, *when*. Sorry, slip of the tongue."

"Okay, so where are we going?" he asked. "And *don't* say the diner, or I'm ditching you."

I laughed, all my nerves spilling out. "You're *ditching* me?" I tugged on the ropes that held us together. "Where are you going exactly?"

"We're not going to the diner for a date," he said firmly. "That's a casual *lunch* spot, not a *date* spot."

"Fine," I conceded. "*You* plan the date, anything you want. Within reason."

"What does *'within reason'* mean?" Dean clarified, like I knew he would.

"No crossing state lines or anything that costs over a hundred dollars. And no suits."

"*No suits?*" Dean asked, appalled.

"For me, I meant. You can wear whatever you want, you always do. But I'm not going anyplace I have to wear a suit."

"Fine, deal."

"Okay." It was a good thing Dean couldn't see my face. I was sure I was red as a tomato. I couldn't name the last time I'd been on a date—a real date. I hadn't even thought about dating after Malcolm left, and the last time *we'd* gone on a date was...I couldn't even remember it had been so long.

"But first we have to get out of this," I said, refocusing. "When they come back, get them talking. They were fighting earlier when I got here. Maybe we can tug on that thread, get them to turn on each other."

Dean chuckled. "You really do get all your ideas from movies and books, don't you?"

I frowned. "Shut up, it could work!"

"Okay, I'll try. Don't help too much, though. You tend to overact."

I scoffed. "Me? *I* tend to overact? Mr. Theater-kid-know-it-all?"

He laughed through his nose. "Why do you keep bringing that up? Do you have something against theater kids?"

"No," I said reflexively.

"*Ah*, so you *wanted* to be a theater kid, and you're jealous of me because you never got the chance?"

I snorted. "That's not it either."

But Dean wasn't buying it. "Sure, okay."

A rustling at the back of the stage cut our conversation short. Then Jake was laughing. He walked out from behind the back curtains holding a packet of papers in his hand. He was smiling from ear to ear. Robert followed right behind and grabbed Jake's waist with a devilish grin.

"Having fun?" Dean asked dryly.

"It took me a few days," Jake started, "but I finally found that stupid will. I hadn't realized that Caroline was such a paranoid witch."

Robert tutted his tongue. "Don't speak ill of the dead, Jake, it's tacky."

"Where was it hidden?" I asked, partially curious, while also trying to keep them talking.

"It was in Robert's office, if you can believe it," Jake said. "Hidden in plain sight. She hid the damn thing right behind his framed poster of The Phantom of The Opera."

"She was taunting me," Robert added. "Putting it right in front of my face, but somewhere I'd never see it."

"Caroline was clever," Dean said, a hard edge to his voice. "That's something I always admired about her. She always kept you guessing."

"Yes, I'm surprised she never caught on about you two," I said. "How *did* you lovebirds meet anyway?"

Jake smiled and pulled Robert in closer. "We met at an open casting for the last production Robert put on. It was love at first sight."

Robert laughed. "Well, not initially. I thought you were kind of a brat, coming in with so much attitude. But you were by far the most talented person I'd seen all week. Slowly, you grew on me."

Jake rolled his eyes and said, "And then late rehearsals got longer and longer."

"And the rest is history," Robert finished.

Their lovey-dovey aura disgusted me.

"So what are you going to do with your millions?" I asked, steering the conversation. "If the cops don't catch you first, that is."

Jake grinned, revealing bright white teeth. "Oh, they won't. No one suspects either of us. Heather was the *perfect* scapegoat. That idiot detective believes it was all her. That she planned everything."

So they were going to frame a dead girl who couldn't defend herself. Classy. Just as I had predicted.

"Yes, how *did* you do it? I understand the basics, but how did you get Caroline to swallow all those pills?" Dean asked.

Jake laughed. "Easily. Caroline was a drunk," he said, venom lacing his words. "After she let me in it wasn't hard to convince her to drink a bottle of wine, then a second one. At that point, putting the pipe down her throat and feeding her the pills was a snap."

So it was as I'd suspected: Caroline had let him inside, and after she was wasted he force-fed her the pills and dumped her into the pool.

"But how did you get away from your friends?" I asked. His castmates had confirmed his alibi that he was at the club with them all night. How did he manage that? Were they lying for him?

He smiled. "That part was fun. I told one of my friends that I had a trick who wanted to mess around in the alley behind the club. He covered for me while I drove over to Caroline's and back. It didn't take long. Under an hour. Nobody questioned me at all. They were too drunk to even notice I'd been missing. I made sure of it."

Ah, so that explained it. Time had a way of bending when you were inebriated. An hour on the dance floor could have felt like ten minutes to them.

"And Heather?" I asked.

"That was me, actually," Robert said, taking credit. "She was a sweet girl, really, but she asked too many damn questions. And then she hired the two of you behind my back?" He shook his head. "She had to go. She was such a wreck after Caroline died, it wasn't a stretch to paint her as the killer. You saw it, that Detective Warner bought everything."

"Yeah, he's not too bright," I agreed. "But how are you going to explain Kirk getting attacked? Or the theater being ransacked? You've left so many threads behind."

"You're right," Jake said, turning to Robert. "Which is why we need to get rid of *all* the evidence. Every last piece of it."

Robert frowned and crossed his arms. "I told you *no*, Jake. I can't believe you're even considering it."

"Robert, it's *perfect*." Jake grabbed Robert's shoulders. "Why can't you see that? If we burn this place to the ground, it solves all our problems, and we can use the insurance money on top of the inheritance to start over again."

Robert narrowed his eyes. "I don't want to start over. I've put so much into this place. *So much*."

Jake rested his hand on Robert's chest. "I know that, baby. But think about the bigger picture. The Marching Cry can be the biggest show in LA if we play our cards right. This doesn't have to change anything."

"He wants to destroy your legacy?" Dean said quietly, almost as if to himself.

Robert groaned. "*Agh*, I can't do it. Let's just kill these two and drop them in a ravine somewhere. The cops will never find them. We don't *need* to start all over again."

"Robert," Jake started, his voice dropping. "It's just a building. The theater is inside both of us."

"Wasn't this place built in the 1920s?" Dean said to nobody in particular. "So much history."

"Shut up!" Jake barked, rearing his head in our direction. "I can see what you're doing, and it's not working."

I wasn't so sure about that. Robert looked conflicted. "We'd have to delay the show by at least a *year*, Jake."

"So we'll work even harder." He nodded. "We've done it once, we can do it again. Come on, Robert. This is our best shot to freedom. The cops will never question finding these two among the rubble. They were poking their heads in where they didn't belong, and the police already know they were harassing you."

I watched as the machinations behind Robert's eyes turned. He spun and started pacing the length of the stage, his shoes tapping against the wooden floor. He was quiet for a full minute before he said, "Fine, but I don't like it."

Jake pouted his bottom lip. "I know, baby."

Watching Jake call Robert *baby*—who was twice his age—made me sick. They'd killed two people, and were attempting to kill us again, just for a theater?

"The show must go on," Robert said, which worried me. That didn't sound like he was on our side anymore.

I bumped my hand into Deans behind my back and his fingers grabbed at mine. We'd never held hands before, however this seemed like an appropriate moment.

Jake pulled out a lighter from his pocket and flicked it a few times, testing the flame. "We'll need some accelerant, but it has to be something plausible. We need this to look real. It has to stand up to investigation." He looked up past the stage. "Harrison is always complaining about how those old lights are going to start a fire one of these days. That's perfect."

Holding Dean's hand, something occurred to me that made me want to shout with how stupid I was. I traced each of Dean's fingers until I caught the ring. He was wearing it! My gift. I couldn't reach far enough to pull it off, the angle wasn't right. I trailed the outline of the ring and tapped Dean's hands.

"What?" he whispered.

"*The ring,*" I said insistently, hoping Robert and Jake were too distracted to notice we were talking to each other.

"What about—" The question died on his lips as he remembered. "*Oh my God.*"

"Yeah, get to it, please."

He released my hand, and I felt the soft vibration of movement as he expanded the blade from the ring and started sawing into my bindings, unable to reach his own.

I just needed a *little* give, a *little* slack.

258

Jake looked up toward the rafters and the catwalk. "If we drop one of the lights from there and make sure the wires stay intact, we can add a little kindling on the stage to ensure it ignites, and the stage should catch easily. This whole place is covered in stains and flammable varnish." He grabbed some prop newspapers from a cart to the side of the stage and placed them in a pile on the floor. "I just need to open the curtains so they don't stop the flames." He ran off upstage.

"I'll go and unfasten the light," Robert said as he headed toward the stairs.

"We don't have much time," I said at full volume now that they were gone. "How we doing?" I tested the ropes by twisting my wrist just slightly.

"This is a *very* small blade, Noah," Dean said through gritted teeth.

"Well how much do you want that date?" I asked, taunting him.

The intensity of his sawing increased, which normally would have made me laugh, but here and now, I was too stressed to find anything funny. My hair and forehead were damp from the hot stage lights, and my heart was beating heavy in my chest. I was keenly aware of the sharp blade mere centimeters from my flesh.

"Almost got it," Dean said through a heavy breath.

The curtains started to pull apart, revealing the empty audience. We only had seconds left.

I wriggled my wrist once more. There was slack this time, just an inch of it. "*Okay*," I snapped the rest of the thick cord and felt a scrape on my arm.

"Shit, did I cut you?"

Blood dripped down my wrist, but I didn't care. I knelt down and furiously untied Dean's bindings. They were tight, but luckily I'd made a few knotted friendship bracelets with Lexi when she was younger. The knots were no match for me. Dean yanked his arms free and scrambled from the chair just as the spotlight came crashing down from the catwalk onto the stage, cord and all. A spark was all that was needed, a surge of electricity. The fire started in the center of the stage, small at first, though it quickly grew, eating up the Turkish carpets and surging toward the auditorium.

"Let's get out of here," I said, pulling Dean forward.

Robert's voice shouted from the catwalk, "They're getting away. Stop them!"

Jake, who had vanished, reappeared to our right down by the front row of seats.

"*Go! Go!*" I shouted before remembering Dean's knee was in a brace. I looped my arm around his back and shouldered him as we ran up the aisles toward the front of the theater. Whatever set pieces and furniture that had been behind stage were now on fire. The flames grew, reaching higher and higher. We needed to get out of here. Dark, noxious smoke began to fill the space. I covered my mouth with my hand as we reached the top level of the auditorium and dashed down a hallway, Jake at our heels.

"Come back here!" he shouted. Did he really think that was going to work?

"No thanks!" Dean retorted as we reached one of the emergency exits and burst out into the alley beside the theater. The skyline was orange and pink—golden hour.

We were safe from the fire, but not safe from Jake. He rushed out the exit behind us, his eyes ablaze. "Why won't you two just die already?" He pulled a pocket knife from his jeans and clicked it open. It was long and sharp.

"*Because I don't want to!*" Dean shouted defiantly. Now was *not* the time or place. My private investigator course teacher had always drilled into us: a gun meant charge them, a knife, however, meant *run*. I dragged Dean down the alley toward the busy boulevard. He tripped on a crack in the cement and pulled us both down. The stone bit into my palm as I braced our fall.

"Shit." I grabbed Dean's waist and launched us into a run again. We crossed the street just as a taxi was pulling up to the theater. Jake bounced off the hood like a rag doll, stopping us in our tracks in the middle of the street.

"Oh shit," Dean whispered.

The passenger jumped out of the back seat of the cab—it was Lexi of all people. "Oh my God, did I kill him?" she shouted, her hand covering her mouth in shock.

"Dean waved his hand lazily, struggling to catch his breath. "Don't worry, that was the bad guy."

She put her hands on her hips. "Oh...good."

The taxi driver hopped out and stared at Jake's limp body. He didn't look so convinced.

Jake wasn't dead, but certainly injured.

"I already called the cops," Lexi shouted as people on the street began to stop and shout, pointing at the theater. Flames were licking the walls of the interior as the fire spread.

"What about Robert?" Dean asked. "Do you think he's still inside?"

I searched the faces of the people in the street. He wasn't among them. "I don't know. He must have gotten out. He had time." So why wasn't he here? Crouching over his injured boyfriend?

The sound of police sirens grew louder as red and blue painted the darkness.

"I can't believe we got out of there," Dean said.

Lexi ran around the car and hugged us both close. "Are you guys all right? You didn't text me back, and I got worried."

"Thanks, kid. You just saved our lives," I said.

Dean laughed. "In more ways than one," he said, pointing at the cab next to Jake's groaning figure.

"Should we help him?" Lexi asked.

"Nah, he's fine," I said. "Just a little bruised."

* * *

When the police finally arrived, an ambulance took Jake away in handcuffs, and Warner took us downtown to talk. Three firetrucks were putting out the flames from the theater as we were driven away. The brick looked intact, but, no doubt, the inside was collapsed and destroyed beyond repair. My heart went out to everyone that had worked there. They were just caught up in this game of Robert's—innocent bystanders. Sort of. Kirk and Tim were still blackmailers, but other than that, the rest were innocent bystanders.

We had to walk Warner through the case like a child, step by step. "So Robert *wasn't* in love with Camilla?" he asked near the end, his brows in a constant furrow.

"It was a cover, just like Jake with Caroline ," I said. "Camilla had no part in this, trust me."

"And Robert and Jake were...*together*?" Warner looked as confused as I'd felt a couple hours ago.

"Turns out, love really is blind," Dean joked.

Warner and his team had ignored a lot, however they couldn't ignore a burned out building and Jake attacking us with a knife. Then there was the whole knocked-out-and-tied-up to-a-chair thing. So the pair was going down for murder, attempted murder, arson, breaking and entering, and a whole host of other crimes.

Robert was still missing. The cops had searched the downtown Hollywood area and hadn't caught up to him yet. They would. He couldn't get out of town without *someone* spotting his face. He'd, no doubt, be on the morning news and all the papers thanks to a tip from me. I had close connections to the LA times. I even had Adeya Nwadike reach out and agree to run a piece online slamming Robert. Glad she was using her scorn for good use.

Once Warner finally let us go, I drove Dean back to his apartment. Lexi had gone home early to avoid her parents, and I didn't blame her. Being at the scene of a crime kinda broke her curfew.

"How's your knee?" I asked as I parked in front of the apartment building.

Dean shrugged. "I'm fine. My suit on the other hand..." His pale blue suit was a little scuffed around the edges from all the running and fighting.

"I'm sorry."

He nodded slowly. "How about your arm?" The paramedics had patched up my forearm on the scene right before we left.

"It's just a scratch," I insisted.

"Are you sure? Let me see it."

He wouldn't take no for an answer, so I peeled off the bandage. The scratch was long, but not deep enough to need stitches. It had only bled so much because of its location.

He took my arm and inspected the wound. "I'm sorry."

"You *saved* us," I countered. "Don't be sorry."

He leaned down and kissed my wrist, his soft lips sending tingles up my arm. "There, all better."

I laughed. "*Not* all better, you just infected my wound. Now I'm going to die of sepsis."

He knit his brows together. "Take it back. I can't go home if I think you're going to die in your sleep."

"Fine, I take it back." I grinned. "It's all better now. Thanks."

He smiled, his dark eyes turning golden in the lamplight "Good." He lingered, gazing at me. This was the part where he was supposed to get out of the car.

"What?" I asked.

He didn't look away. "You're so handsome, Noah."

"*What?* No, I'm not." My cheeks immediately burned from the compliment. I was *okay* looking, but no one would ever call me *handsome*.

"Yeah, you are. You can't help it." He leaned closer across the center console. "Can I kiss you?" He was mere inches from me.

I nodded reflexively, and his lips brushed mine, soft and tentative. It mirrored our first kiss in so many ways. He pulled away and opened his eyes.

"Why are we always kissing in cars?" I asked.

He shrugged and smiled. "I don't know. Want to come inside?"

I shook my head. I wasn't ready for that. This was already too much. "You need to rest," I argued lamely.

He rolled his eyes. "So do you, detective. But okay, I'll go. Just don't forget about your promise." He opened the car door and started to get out. "We got a hot date on Saturday."

"Saturday?" I gulped.

"Eight o'clock. Dress casual." He almost closed the door and then turned back. "But not *too* casual, you know? It's still a date. Don't wear your work clothes."

I laughed through my nose and smiled. "I won't, I promise."

"Okay." His gaze lingered on mine for a second before he closed the door and walked up the steps to his apartment.

A date. With Dean. *What have I done?*

TWENTY

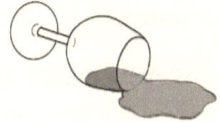

I set the cardboard box on the floor by my bed and started sorting through the pile I'd gathered. One pair of Malcolm's sneakers. One pair of his old sunglasses he never wore. The bright red Hawaiian shirt he got me for my birthday when he told me I should be more bold. A stack of tacky crime books I'd roll my eyes at every time I caught him reading one. Two pairs of old pajamas he'd left behind, a stack of old letters, and...the ring.

I held the ring in the palm of my hand. It was a simple gold band. Something you could find at any ring shop. It had been sitting on my bedside table in a little dish for the last six months, taunting me. Every day I had the strange urge to slip it on until I'd catch myself. Malcolm was gone, yet I was still living with his ghost. All his forgotten things, as if he was going to come back for them. He wasn't. He'd made that pretty clear when he finally left after a *particularly* loud fight. And all this time I'd allowed myself to become one of his forgotten objects. Waiting for his return.

I dropped the gold band in the box and folded the top closed. No more waiting around, no more holding back my life. It was time to move on. I labeled the box for donation and dropped it outside my front door to take down later. My bedroom felt suddenly fresh. Like my hasty, imperfect buzzcut, the apartment had been just slightly off since Malcolm left, but now it was time to regrow, to reorganize, and—if Lexi and Dean had their way—redecorate.

Today was Saturday. The day of the infamous date that Dean had bargained for. I kept telling myself that it was a terrible idea. We worked together. What if it all fell flat? What if we learned too much about each other and realized we weren't compatible? After all, I'd *just* cleared out Malcolm's things. Was I even ready for this? Would I *ever* be ready for this?

I'd decided against telling Lexi about the date. I didn't need any more pressure, and if it went badly I didn't need that either.

I pulled out my best pair of chinos and a dark henley from my college days that was slightly too small. Was this good enough? There wasn't anything to be done about my hair, which was still too short to really style. I'd grown accustomed to the length and was considering buzzing it again. It was so economical/practical since I could do it myself. And I needed to save the money considering both our clients in this case had died. Who was left to pay us? Not that I'd needed to be paid. We would have solved the case no matter what, for both Caroline and Heather. They'd deserved so much better.

A splash of cologne and my better pair of boots and I was ready to go. Captain was excited, as if he could feel my manic, nervous energy—his tail wagging and his tongue hanging out. I scratched his chin and gave him a bone to gnaw on while I was gone. "Be good, boy," I said, though he was always good.

Dean insisted on keeping every detail of the date a surprise, adding to my nerves. I didn't know what Dean's idea of a date would be. Hopefully not clubbing downtown or something else out of my wheelhouse.

Also, funny enough, since Dean no longer had a car, *I* was driving him to my own surprise. I picked him up from his apartment in Northeast LA. He was wearing a very subtle gray suit set that had flecks of red woven into the fabric. His chestnut hair was parted and slicked back as usual, and he'd elected not to shave, so he had a fine layer of dark stubble along his jaw. He looked amazing. "Nice suit," I said as he slipped inside.

He grinned a boyish smile. "Thanks, ready for the best date you've ever been on?"

I chucked. "Wow, really upselling yourself, aren't you?"

He shrugged. "What, do you want me to lie?"

I loved how confident Dean was. It was a great quality for a detective, though it could also get you into trouble quickly if you weren't careful.

"You look nice as well," Dean said, his eyes trailing my figure. "I didn't know you owned a henley."

I pinched my brows. "Why would you? Are you cataloging my closet or something?"

He shrugged, not exactly saying *no*. He leaned in and kissed my cheek. "And you're wearing the cologne I got you."

I flushed. Of course he'd notice. He noticed everything. "Yep, so where we heading?" I asked, eager to change the subject.

He listed off an address, and I started driving. It was a spot not too far from us in East Hollywood. When I pulled up and parked, I was confused. The building didn't have a sign, it couldn't be a restaurant. "What exactly are we doing here?" I asked.

"You'll see. Come on, scaredy-cat. You can go toe-to-toe with murderers, but you're afraid of a little date?"

If only he knew how right he was. Hit the nail straight on the head. I cleared my throat. "I'm not afraid, just confused."

Dean got out of the Jeep and forced me to follow him. Inside the building was a small white lobby, and behind a partition that cut the space in half was a full commercial kitchen. I was more confused than ever. A woman walked out from the back, wearing a blue apron. She had her dark hair up in a ponytail and a smile on her crimson lips. "Hi, you two. Did you find the place all right?"

Dean nodded. "Of course. This is Noah, and I'm Dean."

She walked over and shook our hands. "I'm Marissa Lee, I'll be your instructor today."

"Instructor?" I asked.

Dean nodded eagerly. "Yes, *surprise*. I booked us a Korean cooking lesson."

"*Oh.*" I *was* surprised. I didn't think Dean remembered our conversation about my grandparents' restaurant.

He narrowed his eyes, trying to gauge my reaction. "Because you said you always wanted to learn, but never got the chance."

I smiled. "I did. You're right. This is perfect."

Marissa looked between the two of us and grinned. "You guys been dating long?" she asked, which made me laugh.

"Uh, first date," I said.

Dean cocked his head to the side. "But don't worry, we already know each other. Imagine a blind first date trying to learn to cook with a stranger."

I laughed through my nose, imagining it. "If I didn't already know you I think I'd want to skewer you."

He chuckled. "Stop, that's mean."

Marissa smiled at our banter and reached across a metal counter to grab two identical aprons. "Here's your aprons. Let's get our hands washed and then we can start."

"What are we making?" I asked, still out of the loop.

"Kimbap," Dean replied.

I'd eaten a million kimbap, it was a staple at any Korean event: a picnic, a field trip, a holiday lunch, anything really. Except, my mom had always *bought* her kimbap after my grandparents passed. I'd never seen it made before.

As it turned out, I was kinda good at cooking. I still didn't trust Dean with a knife—it worried me, but he seemed to know what he was doing. He prepped the veggies, and then Marissa and I sautéed them.

"Hey look, a vegetable," Dean said as he watched me sauté some carrots. "Been a long time since you've had one of those, huh?"

I gave him a dirty look. "Shut up, I'm still alive, aren't I?"

Then we placed our fried meats, vegetables, pickled radish, and burdock onto nori topped with freshly seasoned rice and rolled our kimbap. It was very satisfying. I wasn't the best at the rolling part. Mine were sorta lumpy and misshapen while Marissa's were perfectly even and didn't fall apart when they were cut. But she'd had years of practice. I'd improve if I tried again.

After all the cooking, we sat at a table in the front to eat. Marissa retreated to the back of the kitchen to give us some privacy.

"Did I do good?" Dean asked.

I knew he was asking about the date as a whole, not just his kimbap —which looked a touch better than mine, though I'd never admit that to him. "Yeah, you did good." I smiled.

"Were you surprised?" he asked with an arched brow.

I laughed. "Yes, I was surprised. Thanks for not taking me clubbing."

He reached over and patted my hand. "I knew that wasn't really your speed."

I frowned. "Hey, my *speed*? You're only, like, two years younger than me at most."

He grinned and ate another piece of his kimbap. "I'll take you clubbing one day, and you'll love it. You just have to find the right clubs."

I shook my head. "I'll take your word for it."

"So what do we do now? About the case, I mean," he asked. "Did Warner tell you anything else?"

I nodded. "I heard from a cop friend at the office this morning. They caught Robert at the border trying to get into Mexico."

"They did?" Dean laughed. "I guess he wasn't so attached to Jake after all."

"Not so much." I took a sip of water. "Maybe they'll both be in the same prison, who knows."

He ate another piece of kimbap. "And what about the theater?"

I shrugged. "It's destroyed, but hopefully the city will make it a national landmark and get some funding to restore it. Otherwise some land-hungry LA elite will snatch it up, demolish it, and build some cookie-cutter high-rise apartments."

"Hopefully." He swallowed his bite. "And what about Harrison? We were so sure he was the guy because his alibi was crap. Did you ever figure out where he went that night?"

I laughed through my nose. "Yeah, as it turns out he was just pretending to be drunk so that he could ditch his friend to go meet up with a girl in Venice Beach."

Dean frowned. "But why lie about that?"

I cocked my head to the side. "The woman in question was his friend's sister. "

"Oh my."

I laughed. "Yeah. I bet his friend wasn't too happy about that."

"I'd say I felt sorry for him, but I don't. He made our lives much harder than it had to be instead of just telling us the truth."

"Agreed."

Dean wiped his mouth with his napkin "So I saw Kirk before I came here."

"You did?" I looked up. "How is he?"

"He should make a full recovery. The doctor said he only had very minor brain damage. I think he was more upset that his costumes were destroyed than his health."

I smiled. "That sounds about right. Well, I'm glad he woke up. He should be able to testify against Jake during the trial."

He sighed. "So I guess that's it? It's over?"

"Yeah." I laced my hands together across the table. "We caught the bad guys. I thought you'd be more excited?"

He frowned. "I am, it's just, Caroline and Heather are still dead, you know?"

I nodded. I did know. What was done couldn't be undone.

"And we're still poor," he added on, which made me chuckle.

"It's not so bad. We still have coffee," I held up the kimbap, "and good food. We'll be fine."

He smiled. "And you got *me*. I'm not going anywhere. One case solved. Here's to the next one." He raised his water glass and clinked it together with mine.

"On to the next one." I grinned. I found his words strangely comforting. He wasn't going to leave anytime soon. Then a shred of doubt crept up into the back of my mind. That's what Malcolm had said too. And look how that had ended up.

* * *

Two days later I received a phone call from Caroline's lawyer. What he told me was so insane I had to put it on speaker for both Dean and Lexi to hear. "Repeat what you just told me, please."

Mr. Trent—at Trent, McTavish, and Mannheim—cleared his throat and said, "Well as it turns out Caroline's new will *did not* name Jake Amarov as you might have thought."

Dean knit his brows together. "But we *saw* the will. Saw his name."

"Caroline did not have a printed copy of the will. I had advised against that, and she'd agreed with me that it was a dangerous idea. The only copy of the will was here at the office, safely filed away.

"So what about the will that Jake found at the theater that named him?" Dean asked.

I shrugged. "Just a game, apparently. Maybe Caroline knew that Jake was playing her, or maybe she wanted to mess with Robert. I don't know."

"So who *is* named on the real will?" Lexi asked.

Mr. Trent continued, "The will entrusts the entirety of Caroline's estate to go to Heather, her assistant. Since that is obviously no longer possible, the remaining money will be donated to a list of charities she had named. However, a portion of the money will go to her acting CEO at Runway magazine to pay for her dog's continuing lifelong care. I've already reached out to Ms. Crawford, and along with paying for the dog, she would also like to extend a payment of gratitude to you as thanks for solving Caroline and Heather's murders."

"*Really?*" Dean asked.

"Really," Mr. Trent deadpanned.

"We accept," I said before hugging Dean, picking him up off the ground. When I set him down his cheeks were slightly flushed. We stepped away from each other. Whether or not Lexi noticed the awkwardness of the interaction, she didn't say anything.

We'd solved the case, *and* we'd gotten paid.

"That is going to be one *very* rich dog," Lexi said, making us all laugh.

"Yes indeed."

Author's Note

Thank you so much for reading Cheater, Cheater, Pumpkin Eater. I'm a self published author; I don't have the backing of a huge publishing company to help me out. So if you could please leave a star rating and a review, it would mean the world to me. Thanks a million xoxo, Austin Moon.

Rough Waters

What happens when love gets in the way of business?

Berk is about to lose his job. In order to save himself and his expensive f-boy lifestyle he's forced by his overbearing boss to travel to the small, remote Ruby Island. The island is prime real estate for a new multi-story luxury resort.

Will has never left the island. He's been running the Ruby Inn with his aunt since his parents died, and business lately has been poor. When a new lodger comes to stay something sparks between them. That is, before Will realizes Berk is trying to destroy the only home he's ever known.

Can these two navigate the rough waters of love before the inn goes under?

Catch up on the first book in the series!

How to catch a thief in five days or less.

Noah Sun is desperately broke—his detective agency is on the verge of collapse after his fiancé and business partner abandoned him six months ago. So when Dean Prescott, charismatic millionaire playboy, hires Noah to recover a priceless antiquity that was stolen, it seems too good to be true.

What begins as a simple case of theft takes a turn for the worse when the pair discover a dead body at the socialite's borrowed mansion. The two form an unlikely partnership to solve the case before his uncle comes back and discovers his home is a crime scene.

However, as the investigation progresses, the lines between professional and personal blur. Dean's irresistible charm and the undeniable chemistry between them cause Noah to question his integrity—Dean is annoying and bratty, sure, but he makes Noah laugh in a way he hasn't in a long time. The only problem is that his client is keeping secrets, secrets that might just derail the entire investigation.

Can Noah solve the case before Dean's tangle of lies and his own feelings catch up to him?

About The Author

Austin Moon writes swoon-worthy queer romances and twisty mysteries. When they're not obsessing over their latest novel, they can be found crocheting, illustrating books, and cycling around their rainy little town in the PNW. Sip on a matcha latte and curl up with a good book during a thunderstorm for them, why don't you?

Amazon author page: Austin Moon
Goodreads: Austin moon
Instagram: @Austinmoonbooks
YouTube : @ryanwrites
Tiktok: @Austinmoonbooks